HOSPITALITY FOR ALIEN STRANGERS

Stephen P McCutchan

A SciFi Novel About Hope For Civilization

The day they arrived, and a city
had to choose her values.

ISBN2 __ 9798397043656

Cataloging in Publication data block 3
Library of Congress Control Number 4

To see additional material published by the author and to read his twice-weekly blog, go to www.smccutchan.com

Thanks to Damian Mark Smyth for the design and Annie-Rose Groom-Smyth for modelling for the front cover. Thanks to Paige Lawson for your meticulous proofreading.

Printed in the United States of America
Stephen McCutchan, steve@smccutchan.com
www.smccutchan.com

TABLE OF CONTENTS

Look for other publications by Stephen McCutchan by clicking www.smccutchan.com

CHAPTER 1
SAUCER APPEARANCE

No one understood that what took place on that April day in a modest-sized city in the Midwest would impact the whole of creation. People awoke that Monday, April first, and there they were. Like giant circular shadows, at least ten of what would be referred to as Flying Saucers hovered over the city. It was clearly not an April Fool's moment. It was almost as if the visitors had a sense of humor.

At first, thousands of people stared out their windows in horror, then they began to panic and seek shelter—some in basements, others in closets, or in bedrooms. After a couple of hours, people began to realize that nothing was happening except for their mysterious presence. They made no sound, didn't try to land, didn't shoot missiles or flash strange lights. They were just hovering over the city.

People at the edge of the city had another shock to their system. They discovered the city was enclosed in a giant, almost invisible, bubble that rose from the ground and continued over their heads, closing them inside.

Some tried to take a hammer or drill into the bubble, but they couldn't even make a dent. Many called 911, but the line was soon jammed with calls from all over the city. Police and emergency vehicles established that while one could move around anywhere in the city, no one could pass through the bubble and leave the city.

It was almost as if the people were in a fish tank being observed by their new visitors. Yet it wasn't clear whether the saucers held creatures or were piloted by computers.

Communication was the third surprise. Though people could call anyone within the city, no one, official or normal citizen, could connect with anyone outside the city. There was one weird exception. Anyone can access Netflix, Amazon Prime, and other movie channels. Even people who hadn't previously subscribed—except there were no commercials or outside commentary.

Derek Mansfield, the pastor of Walnut Cove Presbyterian church, stood with his wife, Brooke, on their front porch and stared up like everyone else. In his case, he not only was thinking about how to protect his family but, maybe out of force of habit, was also pondering the significance of this event for his faith and the spiritual challenge for the people of the church he pastored.

For two thousand years, Christians have quoted in Corinthians that "God was in Christ reconciling the world to God-self and not counting their sins against them." If they were about to experience living proof that there were forms of life in other sections of the universe, how is God operating in the rest of the universe?

In another section of the city, Mayor Eleanor Briggs also pondered how she should respond. What is expected of a mayor when the city is invaded by creatures from outer space? She didn't believe the instructional booklet had been written for that scenario.

As a young adult, Eleanor had learned to project an image of calmness in the face of crisis. As a person of color, she had frequently faced prejudice, both personal and systemic. She refused to give people the satisfaction of seeing how they affected her. If she appeared shaken, people would immediately dismiss her as weak.

Eleanor knew that it was always an issue of power, whether personal, institutional, or economic. If they chose how she would react, they were in charge. It often frustrated them when she calmly stood straight and waited on their second or third response.

As she drove to her office, she watched the thin, slow traffic. Occasionally someone would be a daredevil driver or run a light and cause an accident, but most people acted as if they were in a parallel universe. Everything looked the same, but nothing was the same.

She recalled a poignant moment this morning. Her husband, Carlton, kept reaching out to touch her to make sure she was real, then smile shyly, glance up, and shrug his shoulders.

Just before she left for work, he took her by both shoulders and said what she most needed to hear. "I can't say I'm glad you are mayor at this time, but I can't think of anyone who can do a better job handling this craziness. You know you can ask me to do anything to help you, and I will do it."

CHAPTER 2
WE FELT THE BREEZE

It took almost six months for the people of Walnut Cove to verify that the Saucer imprisonment was not unique to them. People had tried all sorts of schemes to break through the bubble that isolated them. Some tried to drill under the invisible shield, only to find that the barrier descended deep within the earth, and all their drills were like toys that broke upon contact.

About six months into the isolation period, a local news studio gathered several city leaders for an interview. DeWitt Freeman, the head of a construction company in the city, was included in a panel. When asked what he would advise, he responded: "Let's stop fooling around,"

When the host of the program pressed him further, he responded: "I was in charge of the use of explosives in the military. I use them all the time in my construction business. You give me the proper explosives; I'll blast a big enough hole in that bubble that you can drive a Mack truck through it."

A Council member, Jess Franklin, who had assumed command of a task force to achieve communication outside the city without success, looked at him with a small glimmer of hope. Jess had always been an activist. He rose in business because he was not afraid of making hard decisions. He may have been under six feet, but when he spoke, it was with authority, and people paid attention.

As they left the studio, he turned to DeWitt Freeman, addressing him by his nickname. Dunk. "I'm interested in your idea, Dunk. Why don't we explore it together with a few colleagues this afternoon? Can you be at my office around 2 pm?"

Dunk was a hulk of a man, two hundred and fifty pounds of hard muscle packed on to his six-foot two frame. He saw Jess Franklin as a no-nonsense decision-maker, and he felt a surge of hope run through him as he turned to Jess and said, "Sure, I'll meet you there."

Jess arranged with the mayor to have council members present to hear DeWit's proposal. At that meeting, Dunk shoved aside any nervousness about talking to some of the power figures in the city. If there was an opportunity for him to act, this was the moment. Building on his TV interview, he challenged these city leaders to take action..

After hearing his presentation, Jess wasted no words. "Let's put it this way, Dunk, if you can find a way to break through, I'll give you $50,000, but if you fail, you owe me $5,000. Now, do you really think you can do it or not?"

"I once busted through a whole mountain, Mr. Franklin. You

help me gather up the explosives and some men, and we'll bust the hell out of that bubble."

Jess turned to his associate, Phil. Give him anything he wants, and let's see if we can break through before I lose my mind."

"Wait a minute," said Eric. "I want to bust out of here as much as anyone, but we don't know what will happen if we manage to get through."

"What are you talking about?" Jess demanded. "What can be worse than being locked in here?"

"What if he cracks the bubble, and it all falls in on us?" asked Antonio.

"Or maybe we cross the line, and the saucerites conclude we aren't worth the trouble, so they blast us to smithereens and prepare to repopulate the earth without waiting any longer," said Kara.

"What do the rest of you think?" asked Mayor Briggs. "We may be playing with more than just the fate of this city."

The debate grew rather heated for a while, but after another hour, they agreed to design an explosive package to be placed on the nose of their most powerful missile.

Dunk immediately put the plan into action.

The mayor announced on the next newscast that the lift-off would occur on the morning of the 14th of September. The whole city was excited that some definite action was finally being taken.

On the fourteenth, the whole city was tense. Since communication was clear, everyone tuned in to a set of reporters who were filming the preparation.

A section of the city was evacuated. Duncan had set up an observation tower from which he could command the operation, and officials could observe.

Some people prayed. Others got drunk. Many just held their breath and stared at their iPad or cell phone.

Derek and Brooke held their two children in their arms.

"It's OK, Dad," said Felicity. "At least we are together, and if the bubble falls in, I've got my kite, and I'm going to fly it so all the world can see what's happening. I've even written my message on it."

"What's your message?" asked Brooke.

"I told them that whatever happens, God is still in charge. We just have to trust God."

Derek's arms shook a little as he saw a tear go down Brooke's cheek. "Thanks, Felicity. We needed to hear that right now."

"OK," said Barrie, "whatever is going to happen is about to happen. He's started the countdown."

"If this works," said Jessie in the control tower, "I swear I'm going to start going back to church."

Eleanor chuckled, "Perhaps you shouldn't combine those two ideas."

"What are you talking about?" growled Jess.

"Somehow swearing and going back to church sound a little in tension with each other."

Before they could continue, the countdown ended, and Duncan pressed the button with his own prayer.

A missile with its explosive nose package lifted off its base and headed toward the top of the bubble.

People were glued to their TVs or iPads in every section of the city. They watched in awe as the missile continued to ascend. When it reached what they assumed was the top of the bubble, it was as if a hole had opened to allow the missile to escape. Far out in space, well past where the saucers hovered, the missile head exploded, and the vast space absorbed the shock of it.

As people stared at their screens, they saw three seemingly unconnected events take place. A bird resting on a rock suddenly rose in the air and continued to leave the city air space. Along with it, a child's kite seemed to follow in its wake. And for the first time in a year, people saw a breeze rustle some trees.

At first, people cheered, but then they saw a second bird rise to flight and crash into the top of the bubble.

"Damn," said Dunk, "For a moment there, I thought I could plan on spending that $50,000. Sorry, Mr. Franklin. I guess I thought I knew more than I did."

"Not sure it will do any good," said Jess, "but I'll give you

$5,000 just for the effort. We had hope for a few days, which is worth a lot."

"Let me add to that hope," said Kara. "It didn't last long, but I got connected to a phone service in India for just a few seconds. Something is still working out there."

Jess Franklin spoke in wonder. "They let it out. They just opened a hole and let the missile pass through. Is there anything they don't control?"

"OK," said Eleanor, "back to the drawing boards. You do wonder if anyone else will see that kite and gain hope from discovering that there is more than one city or even one country that continues to exist."

If anyone wondered how the Saucer people would respond to the missile attempt, it was made clear two weeks later. There was an open stadium near the original missile launch. The platform for the observation tower for that launch had been disassembled. Some children were playing in the field when two events seemed to occur almost simultaneously. First, the children were suddenly levitated into the air and were moved to a nearby football field. Their screams transformed into laughter as they rode on their invisible platform and were gently placed on the fifty-yard line.

The second thing that happened was a series of flashes that seemed to project from at least three Saucers. The field in which the children had been playing was suddenly filled with smoke and burning grass. The second one was partially destroyed, but once the smoke cleared, several people re-entered the field and discovered a visual five-year calendar had been burned onto the field. The first-year calendar was clearly crossed out. The final three each had a question mark. It was further evidence that the Saucer people were not oblivious to life, death, and some version of right and wrong.

The Saucer people were saying, “You have about five years to figure this out—Don’t blow it.”

“Is there no end to what they are capable of?” said Antonio. “It’s like we are mere toys, and they are just playing with us.”

In a calm but firm voice, Eleanor responded. “If my ancestry taught me anything, it was always that regardless of the disaster you are experiencing, look for a new possibility. We aren’t done until the last one of us is gone. God is not defeated no matter how strong the opposition.”

“I agree. Considering their demonstration of power, they could have wiped us out, but for some reason or another, we must have something they want, and they can’t get it if we cease to exist,” said Eric.

“Maybe it’s not convincing them of our worth but convincing ourselves,” said Kara.

“Let’s ponder that and meet again tomorrow,” said Eleanor.

CHAPTER 3
DEREK GETS A MESSAGE

If Derek were to describe his preaching style, he would probably say it was largely an ethical commentary on what was happening in his contemporary world. He would base it on Scripture, usually the Gospels, but largely as a jumping-off point or a point of reference.

Most of his congregation would probably identify him as moderately liberal. That is the way he saw himself. There were plenty of issues in society that needed to be identified and analyzed. As he saw it, greed and self-interest governed society too often. His task was to challenge all forms of selfishness and advocate for justice and compassion.

He liked the Scriptures and thought they did a good job of providing stories and passages upon which he could develop his social commentary. He believed in God and thought God had called him to the ministry, but he rarely thought about it beyond that.

He recalled a fascinating conversation with colleagues about how God called people. Most of them agreed that it just evolved out of the circumstances of life. A couple of them were second-career clergy. No one had experienced a burning bush.

"I was doing well in my career as a stockbroker, but there was always something missing," said Richard. "I wish I could say that, like the disciples, Jesus came by one day and said, 'Follow me.' Instead, it was like a growing hunger, and fortunately, my wife encouraged me to explore it further. I did, and here I am."

"My call is a little more dramatic than that," said Sally. "I was in a ski accident that left me bedridden for over six months. That's a long time to lie on your back and think. One of my repeated visitors during that time was the pastor from Fourth Street Methodist. He kept leaving me books to read and commenting on the spiritual life. As I got stronger, I began thinking about what it would be like to always be reaching out and helping others like a pastor."

She looked down at the floor. "I'm not sure how spiritual that is, but here I am."

"From what I hear over at Resurrection Methodist, Sally, they feel very fortunate to have you," said Vernon. "It isn't easy being a pastor these days, but when I get discouraged or overwhelmed, I think about what it means to be called by God. I don't know any of the twelve who thought being called meant you would have an easy life. What they had was a sense of purpose. I think of that old Viktor Frankl saying, 'If you have a why, you can endure almost any how.'"

"That's good, Vernon. I like that. When I get discouraged, I find an opportunity for a two or three-day retreat and really focus on my WHY. I often come back with renewed energy."

What about you, Derek? How do you think God calls us? Any burning bushes in your life?"

"Not really. When I was in Junior High, a youth leader mentioned that I should consider the ministry. I thought that he was such a cool guy that if he thought that about me, I should consider it. There were moments along the way when I had doubts, but every time I'd sway, something would happen, and I'd swing back. I guess I'm what you would call an evolving pastor."

The conversation continued for another hour. They discussed the visitors and how they could help their congregations cope with this eerie presence. As Derek left, he took a short walk through the city park. The city was in a crisis, but he was reminded that his six-foot-three, slightly over-weight frame had it's own crisis. A little exercise might help reshape that twenty extra pounds.

After he had walked for twenty minutes, he took a shortcut through the woods, planning to emerge on the highway. And that's when it happened.

As he entered the woods, he felt a light rustle in the leaves. He knew there was a pleasant park up the path where he could sit and think about what his colleagues had said.

As he stepped into the opening of the small, secluded park, a warmth seemed to surround him. Then he looked up and saw a beam of light descending upon him.

In his mind, he wanted to run, but the light seemed to envelop him, and he couldn't move. He sensed words entering his mind. It was not like someone was speaking to him, but a message seemed to be forming in his mind.

"We are from a faraway planet in the universe. We have come on a mission to find habitable planets. We want to populate viable planets with healthy life forms who must leave their failing planets."

Derek didn't know why, but he felt like he was in an important conversation with the visitors hovering above the city. He tried to form a proper response. "This planet already has all the lifeforms it can sustain."

"That will be a decision of the Universe Council and not you. Your task is to carry the message to the inhabitants."

"That you are going to replace us and colonize our planet? I don't think so."

"We are not asking permission. We are offering one alternative. We will observe you for five earth-years to observe the qualities of the earth's population."

"FIVE YEARS!!!!! What qualities are you looking for?"

It's not what we want to see but what you offer. We will observe how you live your lives and report that to the Council of the Universe, who will make the decision."

"Why me? I'm just a moderate preacher in one of several religions. There are lots of leaders on this planet who know far more than I do."

"People in other places are having the same conversation."

"That's good to know. Can we consult with each other on how best to do what you want?"

"Maybe sometime later. Not now. Now is the time to decide how to communicate your natural worth. The council will review the report we send and determine what will happen."

"What if we don't prove worthy? What happens then?"

"The Council of the Universe wants the universe's worthiest inhabitants to have the highest quality of planets upon which to live. If you prove less worthy, you will be replaced by those who prove more worthy."

"What happens to us?"

We will seek another planet of lesser worth and repopulate you there."

"So why don't you show yourself so people can see you?"

"You are not ready yet. That will happen in time if, what you call people, prove worthy."

Derek stood there, stunned, and wondering if he had a lighthearted moment or even a mini-stroke that people talk about.

Slowly he felt his body come back under his control. He

looked around, but no one was there, and certainly not the light.

He recalled the recent conversation with his colleagues about how God calls us. He looked up into the sky and spoke aloud, although he knew no one could hear him. "Is this my burning bush, Lord? Couldn't you have chosen someone who had a little more power and influence?"

Silence was the only response. He left the park and headed through the woods toward the highway. What was he going to do now?

As he arrived at the highway, he saw a taxi. Sometimes he would take a bus from here, but today a taxi seemed to be a good choice. He had to decide whom to tell and what to do.

CHAPTER 4
A CRITICAL CHOICE BY THE CITY'S MAYOR

When he arrived home, the house was empty. He went through the house onto the back porch and chose his favorite chair to sit and ponder.

First, he had to decide who would believe him if he told them about his experience. He wasn't sure that he believed it himself. Yet if it were true, and he didn't tell anyone, he would condemn them to death without giving them a choice.

People had kidded him about being in the life-saving business. He knew they were referring to eternal life, but now the decision affected this life, and they had only about four more years to decide.

Brooke came into the house and came out to the porch to greet him. "Hey, you, what have you been up to?"

"Brooke, I know this really sounds strange, but do I look OK? Do I feel like I have a temperature or any other strange thing?"

"Derek, what's going on? You are scaring me."

Derek told her, as best he could, about what had happened out in the woods.

"If the last several months had not happened, I might

wonder if you had gone over the edge myself," she said. "But all you have to do is look up into the sky, and there they are. Regardless of what it means, they have finally made contact—we have communication."

"But why me?"

"Honestly, I don't know. There is part of me that wishes they had chosen someone else. But maybe they can read character. I see you as a man with integrity, compassion, and cautious courage. Maybe they can see that too."

He looked up at her as she bent down and kissed him. "They have chosen a good man, Derek. Do what you have to do."

"But what is that, Brooke? Do I go on television, announce it from the pulpit, or go screaming down the street? What?"

"Call the Mayor, Derek. Let her decide." She pulled out her cell and handed it to him.

Walking through the office procedures took a few moments, but soon Derek heard the mayor's voice.

"This is Mayor Briggs. How may I help you?"

"Mayor, this is the Reverend Derek Mansfield of Walnut Cove Presbyterian Church. I need your advice."

"What is this about?"

"I think I've had communication with the Saucer people."

"You've WHAT!"

"I think I know why they're here, but I need your counsel about where I and we go from here."

“I think we should talk in person. Do you want to come to my office, or shall I meet you at your church?”

“Oh, your office would be fine. When should I come?”

He heard her chuckle a little, and then she said, “The only reason I don’t want you to break any speed limits, Reverend, is I don’t want us to be delayed while you explain your speeding to an arresting officer. Get here as quickly as you can. I’ll have someone meet you on the first floor and bring you up to my office.

“And Reverend,” she paused, “I know that prayer is supposed to be your department, but I’ll be praying, maybe even on my knees, that your experience may be the first step to finding a way beyond this nightmare.”

This time, thought Derek, the threat wasn’t to an individual or even a nation but to the whole planet. He drove slowly down 22nd Street towards the center of the city. He was just alert enough to realize that he was in a daze. He gripped the steering wheel and stared out at the street ahead. It was Tuesday morning. There weren’t many cars on the street. The people who were visible were staring at the sky, pointing, and either shouting or crying. Derek doesn’t need to look up. He knew what was there.

He’s a pastor. He laughed as he thought about that. Until the world turned upside down, he would have been seen as a successful, moderately liberal, dynamic preacher in charge of a vital church in town. Now, who knows what success was?

He slammed on his brakes just in time to miss a car that ran a red light and crossed in front of him. Four motorcycles followed with their riders yelling and shaking their fists at the sky. The world was going crazy.

No one has been able to access the internet or listen to news from outside Walnut Cove in the last several months. Some people, trying to leave the city by car, discovered an impenetrable barrier preventing their exit. Two hundred thousand people of all ages and conditions living in a bubble. The air is good, and the supply of food and medicine seems ample at the moment—though who knows how long that will last.

Communication doesn't make sense, either. We can call home on our cell with a clear signal. We just can't call outside the city. We can access Netflix and Amazon Prime for our movies, but nothing that reveals anything happening outside our bubble.

Derek felt certain that the only message received from outside the city was the message he received from those hovering forms in the sky. He had never cared much for Science Fiction, but his son quickly pointed out that those forms were called flying saucers.

Almost with stars in his eyes, Barrie proceeded to retell many of the science fiction stories about invaders from outer space. Some had good endings, and many were disasters. I'd feel a lot better, thought Derek, if I knew how this one was going to turn out.

They can't really be from outer space, can they? Could the Russians have devised a scary new weapon, or has there been a coup in Washington, and our military is exercising its muscle? His mind wouldn't stop leaping from one impossible scenario to the next. He considered himself too logical to consider most of them, but he couldn't escape the fact that some sort of spaceship was there, silently hovering over his city.

God, how are we going to make it through this? He chastised himself for using the word God so loosely. After all, he was a pastor. He should have been more reverent. Though it was a little out of character, he uttered a brief prayer of confession, trusting that the God he Loved would forgive him.

Up ahead, he saw a small crowd standing around Tasty Freeze. He pulled to the curb and exited the car as he heard a loud voice screaming at a clearly frightened server at the Tasty Freeze window. "Listen here, you whimpering idiot. You see those saucers overhead. We can die at any moment, and you demand that we pay for our sundaes. Here, look at this." He pulled out a ten-dollar bill from his pocket and ripped it in half. "We don't even know if our money has any value."

The woman was almost in tears as Derek stepped forward. "Leave her alone," Derek shoved himself between the man and the attendant. The man started to react, but then Derek's next words froze him in his place. "You don't know me, but I'm Derek Mansfield. I'm on my way to see the mayor because I actually had communication with the saucers."

The crowd grew ghostly quiet. Then a teenage boy spoke up. "What did they say? What did they look like? Who are they?"

"I can't answer the last two questions, but what they said was direct and commanding. They said that we have five years left to live, and if we don't shape up by then, they'll remove us and bring in better creatures to live in this city."

There was a corporate gasp and sounds of crying.

"What do they mean that we should shape up?" said another voice.

"They didn't say. I guess they thought we should be smart enough to figure that out. I don't think it starts by scaring this woman and threatening to steal her ice cream, do you?"

"Miss, if you'll fix me a hot fudge sundae, I'll pay you double what you are charging for your service," said Derek.

Some people chuckled, and others voiced their agreement. "People who work as hard as you do should get more pay than I'll bet they pay you to run this place," said another.

Soon the small crowd turned friendly and almost solicitous of the service they were receiving.

Derek returned to his car and drove off with a big smile,

shaking his head in amusement. He heard himself mumble, "Now, that wasn't so hard, was it?"

He thought about something Brooke had said before he left this morning. "If a doctor told you that you only had five years left to live, knowing you, you'd spend those years helping others. Not a bad goal to have, regardless of what those monsters in the sky want or don't want. They're not really in charge. We are."

With that said, she wrapped her arms around his neck and kissed him. "Go get them, tiger. The mayor is waiting to hear how we are supposed to behave. As a pastor, you've been trying to tell your church that for the last five years. Now, you will have the whole city listening."

With that, she shoved him out the door with a big smile.

Now he was driving towards the mayor's office.

Up ahead, he saw a fire truck leave the station with sirens blazing. I guess some things can't be put on hold just because some flying ships are above us.

He was still tense and confused about what was happening, but once again, he took comfort in his wife's wisdom. He recalled a statement from Victor Frankl, a theologian that had meant a lot to Derek. "The last and most precious freedom that you have is the freedom to choose how you will respond." Brooke was right. The creatures, or whatever they are, who are in the flying saucer can't dictate how we are going to respond.

That's a freedom that belongs to each of us but not to them.

The problem is that most people don't even realize they have a choice and act out of fear. That is rarely a good beginning.

He parked the car in the city hall parking lot. If life is going to end soon, at least we can go out living well.

"Hey, mister, you can't park there. That's for government officials only." The uniformed officer glanced toward the sky. "On the other hand, I guess it doesn't matter much anymore. You got some business with the mayor?" Then it was like a veil had been lifted from his eyes. "Oh, wait, you're that preacher who talked to the saucer people, aren't you? I'm sorry, mister, you can go right in."

Derek smiled. "Don't worry about it. You are just doing your job."

The officer continued to look embarrassed. "What do they want? Are they really going to wipe us all out?"

"I don't know for sure. All they said was that we had five years to shape up. What do you think? What would you do if you were to change people's behavior?"

"I'm just a security guard. What would I know?" Then he hesitated. "I sure hope somebody can figure it out. I have a little five-year-old girl. I'd sure like her to be able to grow up and experience the beauty of this world."

Derek looked at him and then spontaneously reached out and put his hand on his shoulder. "I pray that will happen."

The guard hesitated again. “I’m not much of a Christian,” he mumbled, “but I can change if you think it will help?”

Derek laughed. “If we can figure it out, I might come back and remind you of that promise.”

They both laughed as Derek turned and walked towards the building.

When he arrived, he was greeted by the mayor’s associate, who guided him to the elevator. As he punched the button, he said to Derek, “The mayor’s office is on the twentieth floor.” As the elevator rose, the man spoke. “It’s none of my business, but it must be about this saucer mess. I’ve not seen the mayor so energized since this all began. I hope you have some good advice to offer.”

Derek took a deep breath and let it out slowly. “So do I. It is a little hard to determine what is good and bad news these days, but maybe I can help.”

People glanced nervously their way as they exited the elevator, and Derek was immediately taken to the mayor’s office.

The mayor tried to look calm as he entered, but her excitement was hard to mask.

“So, what happened? Did a ship land, or a voice come out of the sky, or what?”

“It’s very strange, and I encourage you to ask all the skeptical questions you can think of. I just want to decide the best way we can respond. I suggest that we sit down. This may take a while."

Derek began to describe what he experienced in the park. "I've never been much of a fan of science fiction, and I am open to the possibility that I hallucinated, but I was walking into that picnic area in the middle of the city park when it happened."

The mayor held up her hand. "Reverend, I will take notes, but do you mind if I also record our conversation?"

"Of course not. Go right ahead."

He paused until she had the recorder running. Then he continued.

"I had just stepped off the path and into the clearing when I felt it. I felt a warmth come over me. I looked up and saw this large light descending and enveloping me."

"Then words began forming in my mind. It wasn't like thoughts, exactly. It was more like words forming into sentences in my mind. But it was more than that. I could talk back—or at least think words back. Soon we were actually having a conversation. I can't say I heard words, but I was clearly receiving a message and allowed to ask questions."

"What was the tone like? Was it mechanical, high or low pitched, rapid or slow?"

"It was moderately pitched but not in any accent I've heard before. There was no rush. And I challenged what was being said a couple of times, and the voice was neither insistent nor offended but kept responding in the same moderate cadence."

Derek paused a couple of seconds. Eleanor leaned forward and placed a hand on his arm. "Go ahead, Derek. Tell me the essence of the message. What is it they want?"

Derek glanced out the window and then back to the mayor, who was leaning forward so far, he feared she might fall off her chair.

"Madam mayor, our visitors are from a planet far off in another section of the universe. Apparently, their life forms are much more advanced than ours, and they have formed what they call the Universe Counsel among several planets in their section of the universe."

"So, it's true. I always thought there must be other civilized planets in that vast universe. We couldn't have been the only planet that could sustain life." There was a sparkle in the mayor's eyes. "Please continue, Reverend."

"Please call me Derek."

"Thank you, and you can call me Eleanor. Please continue."

"Well, apparently, several of these occupied planets, although they have advance technology, are living on planets whose global conditions to sustain life are beginning to fade."

"I guess our capacity to harm the planet that birthed us is not unique to the Earth," the mayor said.

"No, it's not, and several of these planets have banded

together to decide how to respond. They concluded that there must be other planets that could sustain some of their populations."

"And that is the reason for their visit?" the mayor asked.

"It is, but there is a strange, shall I say, ethical twist to their exploration. Most of the planets that can sustain life already have life on them. So, the council determined that when resources are scarce, it is only fair to distribute that scarcity of resources according to the worth of the population. It is sort of like a Zero-sum game. You sort of earn your right to share in the resources."

Suddenly the mayor sat back, put her head in her hands, and uttered a curse. "Won't it ever stop? Even in far-off planets, among life forms completely different from ours, we still play these games that to the victor belong the spoils."

Derek sat silently, looking at the mayor. Then the mayor looked up. "OK, how do they determine who is worthy and who is not?" she asked.

"That's an unnerving part of their message. They said they will observe us for the next five years and then take their report to their council to decide. The voice never tried to define the criteria by which we would be measured."

"You are Presbyterian, right?" the mayor asked.

Somewhat puzzled, he nodded in assent.

"I don't mean to pry, but do you drink? I think I could use a drink right now, but it can be a Coke or coffee if you prefer."

"I do drink occasionally, and I would be pleased to share a drink with you."

An impish smile appeared on the mayor's face as she reached over and pushed the intercom button on her desk. "Marie, I mentioned to you before about setting out some drinks in case it was appropriate. We have had a unanimous vote that we are ready for that drink. Please bring it in under a vow of secrecy that you tried to get the mayor tipsy."

She turned back to Derek and said, "I think we have to decide how to break this news in a way that maintains people's confidence that we are working on their behalf."

"I would suggest that we operate on a couple of different levels. I'm a pastor, and I have begun to think about bringing the clergy together to determine how the church should respond. That, however, is different from how the city should respond. I hope there will be some parallels and ways to support each other, but this shouldn't appear to be a religious tactic."

"We can't keep this news from the people very long," said the mayor, "or we will lose their confidence. Let's begin with the council. Then, based on what they decide, we will have a press conference and share what we have with the city at large.

CHAPTER 5
ACTIVE LISTENING

Derek stepped out onto his doorstep to retrieve the morning paper. As he had thousands of times, he bent, grabbed the paper, and glanced at the headlines. This time he almost stumbled off his steps.

WALNUT COVE CHRISTIAN CHURCHES HAVE BETRAYED OUR SAVIOR.

Some naive part of his psyche had almost hoped that a small blessing of the current Saucer crisis would be that the churches might put aside their differences and focus on the larger issue.

The Walnut Cove citizens were traumatized. Some hid in their homes, others fled to their religious community and fell on their knees. Still, others gathered in bars and drank. Some wept, and many shook but were unable to speak. The longer the Saucers hung silently in the sky overhead, occasionally demonstrating their superior technology, the more people's fear grew.

In extra-large bold print above the center fold, accompanied by a large picture of Walnut Cove True Gospel Church, together with a prominent picture of the church's pastor, was the headline WALNUT COVE CHRISTIAN CHURCHES

HAVE BETRAYED OUR SAVIOR.

He leaned against the porch railing and began to read the article. The story was reporting on a major presentation by the True Gospel pastor, Victor Bible, after an assembly of conservative churches in Walnut Cove.

Bible reported that after extensive research and hours of prayer on his knees, it was made known to him that the Saucer creatures were false prophets sent by Satan to deceive the beloved citizens of Walnut Cove. He quoted from Matthew that Jesus had predicted that near the end time, many would come claiming to be the Messiah and even offer a few miracles as proof of their messiahship.

He referred to the presence of the Saucers and their demand that we prove our moral worth. "We are sinners, saved not by our moral worth but by the blood of Jesus," he declared. "As Jesus said in Matthew, 'Beware, that no one lead you astray. For many will come…many false prophets will arise and lead many astray.'"

"Hear my words. Many of our churches will be gathering in the next few days. They will falsely declare that we citizens can save the city by becoming better people." He continued, "It is abundantly clear that our beloved Jesus was fully human as we are. He performed many miracles and condemned the false faith of the Sadducees and Pharisees. If you truly accept Jesus as your savior, I urge you to abandon these false prophets, return to a true Gospel church, and watch how God will soon destroy these false messiahs."

The article continued for several more columns with variants of the same basic message. The other churches had compromised themselves and sinfully begun to follow their fully human and false distortions of the true Messiah. He went on to condemn not only the churches but also the clergy who had betrayed the faith and compromised with the mechanical gods who hovered above us.

It was clearly a battle cry. The city-wide meeting of the city churches had already been announced and was scheduled at Holy Assembly. He was sure that they would have to readjust their agenda to provide for developing a response to this story.

As he reflected on the challenge that the Reverend Bible presented, a response began forming in his mind. Through his conversations with his colleague, Michal, he was clear that one of the real dangers of what they were experiencing was that many residents were responding as if the Saucer people were gods. Even a few small cults had sprung up, offering prayers to our visitors and begging for their forgiveness.

They were challenged to prove their worth, not to God, but to whoever was piloting the saucers. A major contribution the churches could make was to help make that truth clear. Technology was bad enough, but there was nothing divine about it.

He continued to read the article but didn't find much new. The central message was that the other churches would try to prove their worth and fail. The best thing that they could do was to begin attending The Walnut Cove True Vine Holiness church.

Several clergy had consulted with each other and agreed that they needed to hold an assembly to discuss how they might proceed as a church. They were to meet in a couple of hours at First Christian Disciple. As Derek re-entered his house, he knew he would hear from many of his colleagues today. With this major challenge on the paper's front page, Derek knew their major task was to prepare a response to The Reverend Bible and those who thought as he did. It needed to be a response that prevented the churches from getting into a hopeless tangle of words. This might be a good testimony to the power of Active Listening, Derek thought. Maybe we can use it to our advantage.

As he drove to First Christian for the assembly, he thought about the challenge he felt as a pastor. He considered himself a moderate, rational Presbyterian pastor. When the visitors arrived, he had been at Walnut Cove Presbyterian church for almost five years. For several Sundays, not being sure what the city should do, he preached on some of the issues raised but avoided any specific recommendations.

The newspaper story would certainly affect how the clergy

responded. He had quickly agreed to attend the assembly as a participant. There were other, more influential clergy in the city who would provide the leadership. The assembly hall of First Christian Disciples was overflowing as Derek entered. He took a seat near the rear of the hall. He laughed at himself as he thought about how often he had spoken, sometimes humorously or seriously, about 'back row Christians.' As he sat, he was aware of the hushed chatter from the clearly nervous crowd. He had not been in on planning this conference, but he approved of the church re-emphasizing the importance of faith in the city's life.

Suddenly he heard his name being spoken over the loudspeaker. "If Derek Mansfield is in the hall, we would ask him to join us on the stage."

Derek rose and headed down the spacious aisle. Above the chatter, he heard a strong voice speak above the noise. "That will teach you to sit on the back row, Derek." People laughed, and some broke out in applause. As he moved forward, he could feel how the humor and applause had lowered the tension in the room.

It also felt good that after serving five years at Calvary, many of the clergy in the city at least knew him by name, and many of the moderate to liberal ones both accepted him as a friend and had served on several committees with him. As he ascended the steps, he saw Ralph Bunch, a Lutheran pastor, stepping forward to greet him.

"It's good to see you, Derek. One of our spokespersons, Reverend Tom Baker, was called away on an emergency. I suggested that even spontaneously, you could hold your own. Hope you don't mind."

"OK, Ralph, you owe me a hot fudge sundae, but otherwise, it's fine. How do I fit in?"

"If you remember some of what you said in tat paper on "Thy Kingdom come" several weeks ago in our study group, I think that would be an excellent place to begin. Otherwise, just flow with what the faith says that can help us with our current crisis." He paused, "Oh, and this is an open forum format, so you may be challenged a time or so."

Derek looked at the hesitant face of his friend. Then he held up his hand with two fingers extended. "Two hot fudge sundaes, Ralph. Two …"

"Deal, brother."

The Reverend Lovejoy, the senior pastor of First Christian, approached the pulpit and invited those present to come together in prayer.

Following the prayer, he reinforced the reason for the gathering. "My fellow Christians, we live in a terrible time with our city held hostage by the Satanic creatures that occupy the devilish saucers that hover over us in the sky.

"There is one who is more powerful than Satan who has

defeated death and stands with us, even Jesus Christ, our Lord, and Savior. We have gathered here today to remind ourselves that the same Christ who faced death on the cross and rescued those who were tossed to the lions in the early church; yes, I say that same Jesus stands with us today. Be not afraid. God is with us."

There were several shouts of "Amen, Amen."

Harold Vanburen, an Episcopal pastor, took the mike. "We have gathered a panel of religious leaders to share their perspectives and reaffirm the faith that sustains us. This is probably the most diverse assembly of clergy that has ever come together in this city. Listen to them with respect and trust that if someone is a little bizarre in what he or she says, there will be another one come along to speak the truth as you see it."

The first panel member was Reverend Darryl Frostburg from Christ the Shepherd Baptist church on Barrington Avenue. "I think we should prepare our people for the worst-case scenario. They've clearly come from outer space, probably beyond our solar system. They would have already established some form of communication if they wanted to be friendly."

"What does the Bible say about the responsibility of churches in relation to strangers?" Frostburg asked.

"Can we develop some welcoming process in case they are as nervous about us as we are of them?" a panel member interjected.

"I don't believe that Jesus visited a whole lot of planets. He lived here on this planet. So, these creatures have to be pagan," said another panel member.

The give and take among the clergy was wide and varied. After about an hour, Derek stepped forward. "To be truthful, we are all frightened. The fact that they have arrived and the power to maintain a hovering presence would suggest their technology is likely superior to ours."

Another pastor rose to speak. He was breathing hard, and his face was red. "There is nowhere in the Holy Bible where we are commanded to treat monsters from other planets with kindness and compassion."

"Tell the truth in Jesus' name," said a voice near the room's rear.

Before Derek could speak, the speaker continued. "There is only one truth. That truth is JESUS, our Lord and Savior. I don't mean to be unkind, Reverend Mansfield, but you liberals are always trying to water down the Gospel with your namby-pamby gifts and money. They need to be interested in meeting Jesus, and as the Gospel says, how can they hear the Gospel if there is no speaker? That's our job."

There was a pause. Derek broke the silence. "OK, you have heard a very important message from our neighbor at Table 9."

One of Derek's colleagues on the stage handed Derek a

piece of paper. Derek looked at it and then continued. "David, if I hear you correctly, you are saying that since there is no Scripture that talks about neighbors in flying saucers, and you quote Romans 10 referencing 'How are they to hear without someone to proclaim him,' you suggest that our primary task as spiritual leaders in this city is to proclaim Jesus to our saucer neighbors."

Derek paused briefly and said, "This is David Sterling, pastor at True Vine Holiness, by the way."

"It ain't going to help us to convert our Saucer neighbors," said another speaker, "if we can't even demonstrate how to be compassionate towards our human neighbors."

Derek continued, "What I hope we will all see in this interchange is that our capacity to listen to each other, especially if we strongly disagree with each other, declares a value that Jesus taught us about our true selves. David and I might disagree on several things, but he is a valuable child of God, and we can both learn by listening to each other. Maybe that opens the possibility of the Spirit intervening for us with sighs too deep for words."

David Sterling smiled and saluted Derek as many in the room applauded.

The Reverend Michal Talbert came forward and took the mike. "I would suggest that we take a break and demonstrate what most of our world seems to have forgotten to do—that is, we listen deeply to each other for how we should live as a church, if indeed, as our Lord has said, 'the Kingdom is very near to us.' We are the spiritual leaders of this city. How should we guide our people to behave in the face of these saucers?" Come back together in one hour. In the meantime, there are drinks and snacks throughout this room and in the halls."

They continued their conversations as they moved about the assembly. Differences in opinion were widely voiced. There was no unity, but they were talking to each other.

CHAPTER 6
MEETING AT TACO BELL

After the divisive assembly, Derek pondered the church's place in this experience. He believed that the church had a critical role, but having heard the fractured debate, he wondered whether anyone could pull them together in a united witness.

About a week after the assembly, Derek got a call from Michal Talbert, pastor of the leading African American church in the city and a leader at the prior meeting. "Derek, we haven't been in touch since this nightmare began, but I think it's time for some deep thinking from us church folk. I'd like to talk with you and consider the possibility of then gathering some of the more active clergy for some brainstorming. What do you think?"

"My daughter made an interesting comment right before they pushed the button on the failed missile attempt. She said, 'Whatever happens, God is in charge. We just have to have trust and see.' I tell you, Michal, I about lost it."

"Wow, out of the mouth of babes. Your daughter is a very courageous young lady, Derek."

"Thanks, Michal. It made me wonder if we have all slipped into too much secular thinking. Secular thinking isn't getting us very far. Maybe it's time to start taking our faith to a new level. I'm in. When and where do you want to meet?"

"How about the Taco Bell over on Lancaster Ave. As for when, I'm ready anytime today."

"I've got two emails to send, and then I'm ready," said Derek. "How about we both get in our cars and start heading in that direction? You should arrive a few minutes before I do, so save us a table."

"Let's do it."

Derek hung up the phone. I don't know what we can come up with, he thought, but I'm glad Michal called.

As he left his office and headed toward the car, he chuckled. I wonder if our saucer people have overcome racism and are looking for planets with people who already know how to overcome racism. If so, we may be doomed before we get started.

As he pulled onto the interstate, he again felt overwhelmed by the tasks before them. His famous rejoinder to others who talked that way was to remind them that Jesus started with twelve and had a mission to transform the world. Of course, many would respond, "Yeah, and look how much progress we've made."

His eyes spotted the large Taco Bell sign and turned in.

He saw Michal through the window, waved, and turned toward him as he entered.

Michal was tall and had a strong personality that helped him hold his own in most debates. Today, however, he looked both tired and nervous.

"I haven't ordered except for this Coke. Let's get our food first, and then we can talk."

Neither of them talked much as they waited in line. After they had placed their order, they turned to head for their table.

"Heh, mister, you're the one that the saucer monsters talked to, aren't you? I recognize you from the news," said a man in line. Suddenly, everything became silent in the restaurant.

"I am," said Derek, "and the only thing I know is that the voice from the saucer said that we have five years to prove that we can treat each other nicely and be fair and kind."

"No negotiation," said another man in the line. He had a scowl on his face, and his voice was strained. "Just take it or leave it. That ain't right."

"How do you negotiate kindness?" said Michal. "You are either kind or not."

"Who gets to define kindness?" said another woman in line.

"The person you are relating to," said Derek. "Any person knows whether they've been treated kindly or not."

"I may think I've treated you kindly, but you may have had a bad day, and you are all grumpy no matter what I say," said another.

"That's right," said Michal, "which means that you really

have to pay attention to the person you are talking to."

"Imagine a world like that," said another woman. "I'd still be married if my husband had really listened to me. Do you think those saucer people will treat us like they want us to treat them?"

"I don't know, but I do know that we'll be happier people if we live like that for the next several years."

"That's all it would take?" asked another man. "Well, I'll be damned." Then he hesitated and looked embarrassed. "Well, I don't want to be damned, but acting nice to people shouldn't be too hard."

There was a titter of laughter throughout the room. Then one voice in the rear of the room said, "I wonder why no one ever thought about that before."

Derek and Michal smiled and carried their meals to a table in the back of the room.

"Do you really think that's what they want?" asked Michal as he took a bite of his taco.

"Who knows?" said Derek, "They just said that they were evaluating us to see if they should replace us with other creatures from another planet. It's much better than how Europeans treated either the Native Americans or your people. At least they are giving us a chance."

Michal snorted, smiled, and lifted his coke. "To a better world, whether it be for a moment or several years."

Several people passed by their table and smiled various versions of "Thank You."

Maybe they'll leave us alone after five years if we can do that.

With a shy smile, one waitress came by and set two sundaes down in front of them. "We all just wanted to say thanks for making this the best day in the last month." She quickly skipped away.

Both men smiled and waved to those who were working the counters.

"So, Michal, you suggested this meeting. For that, I'm grateful, but I also want to hear what you had in mind."

Michal stuffed a French fry into his mouth, cleaned his lips with his napkin, and cleared his throat. "I'm not sure where I'm going with this, although the last fifteen minutes have started setting off sparks in my mind.

"We are pastors to some of the healthier churches in Walnut Cove. I don't know about you, but I attribute part of that to a combination of managerial gifts and pleasing people—offering a series of opportunities by which they can live out the best in them and do it with people they like."

"I think you have described the outline of a healthy ministry," said Derek. "But where does that go, and what are the sparks you said are going off in your mind?"

"The question that has been nagging at me is, where is God

in all this?"

"Oh, my friend, this will require more than a brief lunch. But I guess we are Christian, and the heart of Christianity began with sharing some bread and wine—and I suspect a few other elements."

Michal laughed and raised his hand to receive a high-five from Derek.

"So where do we begin?" asked Derek.

"Well, if, as your inspired daughter put it, God is in charge, we need to remind ourselves and our congregations that those in the saucers are not God. We've been caught in a wave of victimhood since they arrived. They are powerful and clever, and many of us may need to die before this all plays out, but we, not they, are in charge of our own responses."

"Our Saucer creatures have given us the challenge to decide how we want to live as humans."

"And some of that definitely does have to change because many of our values and behavior have not reflected the best that is in us," added Michal.

"We have been slaves to the wrong Pharaoh, and circumstances from beyond us have led us into a new wilderness. Like those first Israelites, agree on a set of basic standards about what the rules are, how to defeat the enemies, both poisonous snakes and evil tribes, and what direction is the Promised Land toward which we march," said Michal.

"For the next ten minutes, let us trust that the Spirit, with groans too deep for words, can offer us insight about the next steps," said Derek.

And for any who glanced their way, they saw two large men, one Black and one White, with heads bowed and eyes closed, clasping each other's hands and opening themselves to God.

When they had finished with their prayer, Michal took a brief look at the menu, glanced at the waitress pouring coffee, and at Derek, who was studying his menu. "So, partner, if the world is ending in five years, do we really have to watch our diet or just pay attention to our desires?"

The waitress's hand shook. Her eyes began to fill. "If the world is going to end in five years, then why not have a hot-fudge sundae and tip your waitress about ten times your usual tip?"

Derek spit out the water he was drinking as Michal slapped the table and howled.

"You don't really think it's going to end, do you?" she asked. "I've seen you come in here before. You're supposed to be preachers. Shouldn't you be on your knees, begging God or something?"

Derek looked at her. "You may be right, Miss. But right now, the threat is not God but the Saucer people, and I don't believe prayers persuade them. They say we aren't civilized enough to deserve to survive."

"What if you set up a contest between them and God to see who is really in charge?"

"You may have an idea worth exploring," said Michal. "Why don't you bring us some nice fluffy waffles with lots of butter and syrup, and let us talk about that a little more? Maybe your idea about tipping people more might also be worth exploring."

She grinned, topped off their coffee, and as she turned, said over her shoulder, "It doesn't have to be the full ten times. Four or five times would be welcome."

"She does have a point," said Michal, "We have a whole city that is treating our visitors as gods. How should we expect the churches to behave if we really believe God is God?"

"Well, her idea of setting up some type of contest reminds me of the contest between Elijah and the prophets of Baal."

"It's in the book of Kings, isn't it," said Derek. The question was who the true god is, and the contest was to have each set up an altar and see which God would consume the offering."

"And, if I remember correctly, Elijah won the contest, but then Jezebel set him up as an assassination target. So, in a sense, when God acted on Elijah's behalf, the political powers put a price on his head."

We've been talking about the church needing to pay attention to their own faith, but the story suggests that even if we win, we might lose. I don't like that story."

But would the idea of some type of contest between the Saucer people and the people of faith have some possibilities?" asked Derek.

"In a sense, we already have the contest set up," said Michal. Instead of animals on an altar, we have people gathering in church settings. We have communities worldwide who gather to affirm the value or worth of listening and responding to the Spirit of God. But for many, they don't even think about it in that way.

"I've been trying to think about how our liturgy can help people face this crisis."

"Well, for one thing, every seven days, and more if we want to offer it, they are reminded that they are not totally alone," said Derek.

"And that the Saucer people are not God. Although I hear that some little cults are forming, hoping they can appease our visitors and somehow escape the impending apocalypse."

"Not everyone will be open to it, but can we reshape the experience of praise at the beginning to remind them that God is still God?"

"But that's the point, isn't it? We say we are saved by faith and not by works, but then we judge each other by deeds. Our visitors are playing on our guilt. Down deep inside, most of us feel that if we are judged by our deeds, we don't have any chance."

Michal looked around. "So, in theory, our faith offers us an alternate perspective, but we have ignored it."

"What do you think would happen if people did believe they were valued and loved in a manner that let them learn from but not be imprisoned by their guilt?" asked Derek.

"It would free us to pay attention to people's gifts, and the whole world would be better off," said Michal.

"Given our four-hundred-year history, do you think Blacks could forgive Whites," asked Derek.

Michal looked at Derek for what seemed like an eternity. Then he said, "Some would, and some wouldn't, but a lot would depend on whether they believed the White person had really learned from and repented their racist past. Most of us just want the chance to live into our future and stop needing to be constantly looking over our backs."

"What if a whole community was trying to learn from their past but opening themselves to God's future both for themselves and others?" asked Derek.

"OK, we're going deep now. Expand on that."

"I'm beginning to think that one of our problems in how we practice our faith is that we think and act as individuals. Yet Scripture tells us that we are saved to the Body of Christ. That is a community and not just a group of individuals?

"But to be blunt, the church has a racist past. Even prominent theologians have twisted and distorted Scripture to justify slavery and racism in its many forms.

"So, can a church be saved by grace and not its works? I agree its history is horrible, but so was the history of Israel and the early church if Acts and Corinthians is accurate. But God was not defeated by our sinful history. To paraphrase, God's power has been continually made perfect in our weakness."

"So, do we just ignore the past and pretend it never happened?" said Michal.

"Not sure my people could buy into that," said Michal.

"Not ignore, look for signs of God's grace and learn from our past but not be paralyzed by it. I think Caucasian Christians have much to learn from African American Christians. Our people have been through a four-hundred-year journey of hell, but many used that journey to shape their faith rather than destroy it.

I don't think God sends our visitors to straighten us out, but I do believe that their presence and threat may be gigantic enough to not only capture the world's attention but allow us to experience a major transformation if we are open to it."

"I'm listening," Michal said with a slight edge to his voice. "But I would remind you that we are only two clergy in one city in a very large world."

Derek smiled, "OK, so we only have to find ten more people. Remember, Jesus started to transform the world with 12, and even one of them began by betraying him."

“Point taken, but where do we begin?” said Michal.

“I think the first thing we need to learn as a contemporary church is that we are saved to community and that God’s love and grace are experienced in our relationships to God and neighbor,” Derek said.

“Actually, I’ve had my relationship with God and neighbor tested by the very church you are trying to defend,” said Michal.

“Of course you have,” Derek leans closer to Michal. “That’s where communal confession plays a major role. What if when we approach the time of confession in our worship, we focus our thoughts on those very Christians whose life and deeds have disappointed God, and each of us confesses the sins of our neighbors and they ours? Our salvation is to heal our relationship to God and neighbor, not just some personal cleansing of ourselves.”

“You mean I have to pray for forgiveness for that racist SOB cop who pulled over my son the other night because he was driving in a White neighborhood?”

“Forgive us our debts as we forgive our debtors is how the prayer goes. Who needs to be forgiven by God into wholeness more than the cop you mentioned?”

“My people have been sinned against for over 400 years in this country. I don’t think we need to be a doormat for one more racist cop.”

"Nor do I. Forgiveness doesn't mean ignoring sin. It means praying that God will do what we cannot do—restore the person or, more importantly, the community to what is God's intention for relationships in this fractured world. Would the world be better if that cop was healed by the grace of God and liberated from his prejudices enough to return to your son and offer to make amends?"

"I don't know, Derek. You are asking an awfully lot from a people who have continually been abused."

"And I don't have a right to ask that, but if it evolved through God's grace, the world would be a better place. Our visitors might even see that we are people of value."

"OK, say more about this revised confession thing you are proposing," said Michal.

"I'm just wondering if the prayer of confession needs to be framed less in some generalized statements and more in some directed invitations. For example, what if the prayer was like this:

"God, we gather in thy gracious presence. Probe our souls and lift up any thoughts where any of us felt superior to others because of race, economic status, educational level, gender, etc. (pause) God examine this community and identify any misuse of power, attitude, or status that has distorted the diversity that reflects your love for us. (pause). Lord, liberate in each of us the capacity to reflect the sacrificial love you offer to flow from this community into your hurting world. Forgive us all so we may be the loving community that offers hope and healing."

Before sipping it, Michal lifted his glass and extended a finger to remove some moisture from his cheek. "I can imagine being a part of a faith community that prayed such a prayer on a regular basis. It's asking God to allow us to experience the healing grace that we desperately need."

"I need help from people like you to explore this further. We spoke of needing eight more people. What if we identified twenty more pastors in our area and saw how many of them would join us in exploring how the church can be led by its own faith?

"We don't have the power to convince our visitors any more than those first disciples had the power to change the Roman Empire, but we can try to be more faithful to our calling and see what God can do."

"I'm with you. This will not be an easy journey. Before we get too far down the road, why don't we find a time for our wives to join us for a good meal and get better acquainted? If this works, we will need their support."

"Sounds like an important first step."

CHAPTER 7
THE COUNCIL'S RESPONSE

"All right, just tell me; What in the hell is happening?" Jess was standing in the mayor's office on the twentieth floor of a major office building in Walnut Cove. He was staring out the large window overlooking the main part of the city.

"Less than a year ago, this was a bustling city of 200,000 citizens, and downtown was filled with citizens and plenty of visitors."

He stared up into the sky and paused.

Eric spoke up. "And then they came. Damn," he said, "I don't even like science fiction."

Eric shook his phone in frustration, put it in his pocket, and turned to face the others. "No signal outside the city, and no one in the city knows what is going on. This city is going crazy. This past summer, my family was vacationing at our place on Lake Michigan. I noticed our son, Donnie, was engrossed in a Sci-Fi book. I distinctly remember squeezing his shoulder and saying with a little laugh, 'Why don't you read something more realistic? Can't you find a good book that deals with business, law, or engineering—something you could make a living at?'

"Now we'll be lucky if we even have a future."

Eleanor looked up as Derek paused at the door. "I think I have a little surprise for you."

"Reverend Mansfield. Welcome. We are glad to see you." She turned to the others. "I invited Reverend Mansfield to join us. He has an amazing story to share with us. For reasons he can't explain, it seems like the saucer people chose him to be the first to contact.

"Let's get some coffee and prepare to hear his story."

She turned towards Derek. "Reverend, how do you like yours—cream, sugar?"

"At this point," said Derek, "I think as black as possible would be nice."

"Well, don't keep us in suspense. Are they friendly? Why haven't they communicated yet?" asked Kara."

"I don't have a lot of answers," said Derek, "and the one I have is rather disturbing."

"Listen carefully," said Eleanor. "As strange as it is, what you hear next may well determine the nature of our response as a city."

Derek cleared his throat and looked at the council members, who almost appeared to be holding their breath.

"I know we've all wondered if there are other planets like ours that are populated. If their report is true, there are numerous planets in different sections of the universe. Some residents live on planets that can no longer sustain them for whatever reason. Now they are searching out other planets to inhabit."

"Immigration again. That issue won't leave us alone," said Jess. "I don't think it's too insensitive to just say that, although we are sorry, like the innkeeper told Joseph, 'there is no room at the Inn.'"

"I'm afraid that isn't the question they bring to us. The question is not whether we have room for them but whether they let us stay?"

The members of the council stared at him in silence. Then Kara uttered, "Let us stay? Are they talking about this city, this country, the world, or what?"

"That wasn't clear. They just said we have five years to prove we are worthy."

"Five years until what? It's crazy. We don't know who they are or what they want."

Eric slammed his mug on the table. "Tell me, padre," his bitter sarcasm was thick. "Is this what that Bible of yours says? Are we facing the end of the world, at least as we know it?"

Derek grunted. "I may have missed something, Eric, but I don't recall seeing interstellar saucers in the Bible. That's even more dramatic than a burning bush."

"The Bible is full of unusual events," said Brooke, "but at least except for a few angels here and there, most of what was happening was clearly earthbound."

"All right, everyone," said Mayor Briggs, "Whether they are in the Bible or not, it's pretty clear they are above our city. Many people are hiding in their basements while others are running through the streets in panic. I've brought you together to hear pastor Derek because he was the first to hear a message from our alien visitors."

"Yeah, why did they choose you, Padre?" Eric said as he turned and stared at Derek. "Is this some sort of religious thing?"

"I don't blame you for being upset, Eric, but this is as much a mystery to me as it is to the rest of you."

"How do we know the message is real," asked Antonio. "I think you said that you never really saw them."

"That's right," said Derek. "I just felt their words, but they did respond when I asked them a question. And as for religion, that wasn't even mentioned."

"Maybe the real question is how should we respond if the message is real," said Kara. "How does a city prove it is worthy to survive? At least they put the question to us. We didn't even do that for many of our Native American neighbors."

"All right, people," Mayor Briggs spoke up. "Let's grab our coffee and start thinking. I have a news conference in a couple of hours. We need to give our population some reason to hope."

Antonio, the deputy mayor, watched as the city leadership, who the mayor trusted, began refilling their coffee and taking seats in a rough circle. "Madam Mayor, maybe it's best if we begin by reviewing what we know so far."

Eleanor Briggs nodded and indicated that Antonio should continue.

Antonio pulled out a notebook. "As I have it, on this past April 1st," he snorted and said, 'What an anonymous day,' He looked over at Derek, 'Correct me if I'm wrong, Reverend, but I think you were the first to actually interact with our visitors.'"

"Then you called the mayor."

"Derek nodded. "It was the strangest call I ever made."

Antonio nodded and continued, "Why don't you summarize what you experienced?"

"I had finished coffee with some clergy colleagues, and I decided to take a brief walk in the park and take a shortcut through a picnic area."

"As I entered the clearing, I was thinking about calling Brooke, my wife, and telling her I was headed home. I was reaching for my phone when this strange light appeared in the sky. It was bright, but it was not blinding."

"And that was when you heard the voice?" said Eleanor.

"Yes," Derek said.

"What did it sound like?" asked Antonio.

"I think it was a male voice, but even that isn't clear.

There was no accent that I could detect. Maybe with a little midwestern twang."

"Remind me again of the message," said Jesse. He continued to stare out the window into the sky.

"It was really fairly simple and direct," said Derek. "We are from beyond your solar system and looking for planets that we can populate."

"At first, I thought someone was playing an elaborate April Fool's joke, so I just laughed and said, "That won't work here. We are already overpopulated."

"We are not so interested in your opinion as your behavior," said the voice.

"Then I decided this was serious, so I asked, 'What right have you to take our territory? What behavior are you talking about anyway?'"

They responded, "There are few planets that have the proper conditions to nurture life. Sometimes it is necessary to repopulate with the more civilized beings in the universe. We've done this before, and we've developed a procedure that helps us test the maturity of the population on any planet."

The professor, Kara, spoke up. "Sounds like a colonization procedure—a little like the Europeans and the Native Americans."

"Oh, thanks for the reminder," said Jess. "That's probably one mark against us already."

“More than one, I’m afraid. Don’t forget our slavery experience. As a country, we seem not to do so well in the hospitality department,” said Eleanor.

Kara asked, “Did they spell out what was going to happen? This is really scary.”

“They did say one other thing that I found interesting,” said Derek. “They said that although our history was important, it was the next five years that would be most crucial to the Universe Council’s decision.”

“What in blazes is the Universe Council,” Jessie held up his hands, each wiggling two fingers.

“Maybe it’s like the United Nations but from out there,” said Eric.

“So, our life is in the hands of some invisible strangers that speak to us from the sky,” said Eleanor. “Sounds rather familiar, doesn’t it, Rev.”

“What are you talking about, Kara?” asked Jess as he finished his coffee.

“The Bible,” said Eleanor. “The Israelites hear God speak from the mountain. If I remember correctly, they were offered a whole new way of life, but they had to discover how they would manage that life. They were free to shape their own future, but what they decided affected the future of the world.”

“I’m sure our government will have some more complete information,” said Kara. “Come to think about it, why haven’t we heard from them or any other place? I tried to call my brother in San Francisco, but we couldn't connect. Do you suppose other cities are isolated like we are, and each city must pass the test on its own?"

"And what about other countries? Will they just repopulate the cities and countries that fail their test, or are we all being tested, and the cumulative scores will determine this planet's fate?"

"I hope not," said Kara. "Some of us have some bad history. As was said, this country doesn't have a very good track record regarding the Native Americans and Africans."

"And what about the Asians out west?" said Eric.

"I'm no liberal," said Jess, "but I know enough about that story from my history books to realize if they read our history the same way we do, we may be in deep shit."

"Our shared history is a mixed bag," said Kara, "but if God forgave the Romans after they crucified Jesus, we still have some hope."

"Maybe God is working through our space friends to bring us to our senses," said Antonio.

"Five years is almost a blink in the eye. We've got to have a plan," said Jess.

"While we can't be sure," said Eleanor, "It sounds like even though our past is a factor, it is more important how we live out the next several years. And since we only know about what's happening in this city, I've called you together to begin thinking with me about what we should do."

"I think the first thing we should do," says Jess, "is find out how widespread this is. It's one thing if it is just in Walnut Cove. It is another if lots of the cities in the US are having similar experiences.

"Or maybe all around the world," said Kara.

"That's impossible," said Jess.

"I thought these objects above our city and our living in an impenetrable bubble was impossible," said Kara. "Reverend, I come from a Buddhist ancestry in India and have only been attending a variety of local churches in the city, but I'm wondering could you have a prayer for us?"

When Derek had concluded his prayer, the mayor said, "We'll take a brief break, and then when you are ready, we'll continue the conversation.

CHAPTER 8
BEGIN AT THE BOTTOM

Antonio raised his hand. "Can any of us decide which area of focus interests us?"

"Do you have a particular area that interests you?" asked Eleanor.

"As you know, I am a fourth-generation immigrant from Mexico. I have a booklet that my great-grandfather and grandmother put together telling the story of their journey from Mexico and achieving citizenship in this country. It was a long, dangerous journey, and when they arrived, many people resented their being here and acted in many hurtful ways. We spoke of America as a land of opportunity, but with discriminatory laws and behavior, life was made very difficult for them and their two boys—my grandfather and his brother.

"Yet their eye was on the prize, and they built their own little grocery store in a small community nearby. Eventually, their hard work, very visible participation in the local church, and many acts of kindness to their neighbors paid off, and they were accepted. It's a good story, and reading it makes me proud of my family heritage.

"With the current debate over immigration, it is clear that

many immigrants have not been so lucky. Sometimes it is because of their own failings, and sometimes because of many harsh discriminatory laws, many immigrants end up in prison. In our local prison, over sixty percent of the prisoners are immigrants or people of color."

Antonio chuckled a little, shook his head, and continued. "I'm sure that many of you are aware of this, but at one time over fifty years ago, the city prison was called a reformatory. The idealistic idea was that if someone got into trouble with the law, they would be taken out of society until they had learned their lesson and could re-enter society as a reformed citizen. However, our country eventually grew tired of the effort to reform its wayward citizens and found it easier to just warehouse them instead. That is not just true for immigrants but for other citizens in that prison as well.

"The reason that I raise this is to pose this question. We are trying to demonstrate to our visitors that we are people of worth. I would suggest that our prison system daily makes visible how little we value a significant portion of our population. While I am especially concerned about immigrants, who often lack anyone to stand up for them, it really is true for all those we have chosen to warehouse in our prison.

"Normally, if we were to try to change that system, it would take lots of time and changed legislation. However, one small advantage of our isolation in our bubble is that we can decide for ourselves what changes in this and every area would make a better world. We can implement those changes without the necessity of working through either state or national legislation.

"Hopefully, we will eventually get beyond our saucer challenge, but then we will be able to demonstrate a new way to pursue justice and make some major changes that will benefit prisoners and, therefore, society all around the country.

I assume it is clear, but I would like to be part of the task force that looks at our justice system in the city and with a particular focus on the local prison. I know this is not to be a religious meeting, but let me also remind you that a central emphasis of Jesus's teachings was that he was sent to proclaim release to the prisoners. Wouldn't it be wonderful if we could restore a high percentage of our prisoners to productive citizenship? In the process, we could also save a lot of money used to maintain our inefficient warehousing system.

"OK, I've said my piece and appreciate you listening to me."

The Council stared at Antonio for a few seconds, and then they burst into applause.

"Madame Mayor, may I have the privilege of nominating Antonio to chair the justice task force?" said Eric. "That was a powerful and moving presentation, my friend."

"I doubt any of us want to follow that excellent proposal with our area of interest. I would like you to consider which area interests you and express your interest at our next meeting.

Remember, you don't have to have a solution to the issues raised. That will be for the task forces, which will be formed around the issues to develop.

There was unanimous support for adjournment, and many took the time to give Antonio a big hug and words of support.

A few days later, Antonio took Derek and Eleanor to a meeting that he had arranged with the prison warden. Bryan McPherson. When they arrived, Bryan took them directly to his conference room.

When seated, Bryan said, "Antonio told me what this meeting is about. While I think several details need to be looked at, I don't have any negative thoughts to raise. People have talked about prison reform for years, but I think if we are ever going to do it, our current situation provides us with an opportunity."

"I appreciate your cooperation," said Eleanor. "We hope that by offering our prisoners these opportunities, we will have stronger participation."

"In response to your letter, some of my staff have cleaned up our auditorium, making sure there are plenty of chairs and some tables with water which will be available. If there are other needs, my staff will be available to you.

What we are asking for is fairly simple. We want to identify any prisoner who wants to leave the prison and start a fresh life outside. To do that, the prisoner must be willing to,

1. Name and accept responsibility for their crime.

2. Offer a form of reparation to either the victim or the society around us.

3. Commit to helping another person or group tempted by the same crime.

4. Describe their plan for the reformation of their lives and agree to check in every three months

5. In essence, anyone who is willing to do the work is offered an opportunity for a second chance.

And what if they say they will but really are lying about it?

They will be arrested and charged a second time. They will be sent back to their prison and resume their journey without the necessity of a trial.

Our dream is that it could both lower the population of the prisons and provide individuals with fresh thoughts on how they can contribute to a better life in our city. If their plan is coherent, it will be passed on to the Council for a vote. In many ways, it is a significant opportunity and might reduce some of society's crime.

I realize that not everyone will understand or take advantage of this, but at least it will come closer to demonstrating that in this city, none of us is perfect, and all of us are valuable.

"In response to your letter," said Brian, "some of my staff have cleaned up our auditorium, making sure there are plenty of chairs and some tables with water which will be available. If there are some other needs, my staff will be available to you."

CHAPTER 9
MAYOR'S REPORTS TO CITY

The Council had debated for a couple of hours about what to say at the news conference. They agreed that with the city in extreme panic, it was important that they present a united front and a calmness that none of them really felt.

It quickly became apparent that the normal newsroom would be inadequate, so they shifted it to the assembly hall down the street. Even then, with every reporter in the city, cameras, speakers, and recorders, the room was jam-packed and very noisy as the council entered the stage.

The council quickly took their seats behind the podium from which the mayor prepared to speak.

While Eleanor had disciplined herself over the years to appear calm and in control, even in the worst of circumstances, inside, she was terrified about what would happen.

Derek moved up beside her and spoke softly into her ear. "You will do fine. Let them know the Council, and you are in charge. What you say should be the truth but keep it general and don't say too much."

Then he lightly squeezed her shoulder, stepped back, and resumed his seat near the council members.

There was a slight chuckle. In a firm, calm voice, Eleanor began to speak. "I know that all of you reporters want to provide the best information you can to the people of this city, and since we are both streaming this and broadcasting it on our local channel, we probably will set a record as to the size of our audience."

"I would be delighted to say that what began in this city this past April 1 was a giant April Fool's Day hoax, but I cannot. What we are facing is the biggest challenge that this city, and perhaps this planet, has ever faced.

"The round objects above the city are real, and from everything we can determine, their origin is from off this planet and, likely, from outside our immediate solar system."

There was a gasp from the entire gathering, a few curses, and many who wanted to ask questions.

"I want to provide the city with as much information as I can, and following that, I will take your questions for no longer than an additional half-hour. As you might imagine, we are quite busy.

"If you haven't heard, we have had one brief exchange from what we refer to as our Saucer Visitors. While we can't verify the exchange completely, we are assuming it is authentic until we learn otherwise.

"That communication involved the Reverend Derek Mansfield, who is on the stage with the Council. Neither he nor we understand why he was the message's recipient, but the message was rather direct and clear."

Derek briefly lifted his hand and nodded to the audience.

"It seems that our visitors are from outside our solar system. They represent a consortium of inhabited planets, some of which have experienced significant climate change, rendering their planets unlivable. They are seeking other planets that they might repopulate.

"In examining the challenge before them, they concluded that there is a hierarchy to the quality-of-life forms. They have decided that the higher a life form exists on this hierarchy, the more they need to be provided with a space to live, even if that requires the replacement of the existing population.

"The reason for their presence over our city, and, we assume, other cities as well, is to observe our quality of life and see where we fit in this hierarchy. Once they have observed and measured us, they will report to their Universal Council, who will decide whether we need to be preserved or replaced."

There were more shouts, screams, and curses. Eleanor reached over and picked up a megaphone, through which she shouted.

"BE SILENT, AND I WILL TELL YOU THE REST,"

After repeating that message three times, the room began to calm down so she could continue.

"Obviously, no one wants to hear that we are being observed

and measured. That is beyond our control. The next part of their message is not beyond our control."

A sudden hush swept across the room as they waited to hear what Eleanor would say next.

"According to Dr. Mansfield, our visitors said that they would observe us for five years to measure the quality of our lives. They also said that though our past history mattered, which they could read about in our history books, the real determining factors would be how we lived in the next five years. That is up to us, and your council will be working to help shape our responses, but in the final analysis, it will be up to every one of us."

Eleanor paused, and one reporter took advantage of the moment to present a question.

"Madam Mayor, what you report is totally beyond belief and defies what science has taught us. However, Madam mayor, no one predicted our city would be held prisoner by flying saucers either."

Eleanor nodded and indicated that she should continue.

"The Reverend would know more about this than I would, but this sounds like some apocalyptic scenario from the Bible to me. Is this leading up to some new religious movement emerging?"

"That's so far beyond my knowledge base that I will ask Rev. Mansfield to respond."

She turned and indicated that Derek should come to the mike.

"First of all, in my brief encounter, I received no indication of the presence of faith or lack of it among our visitors. The ethics of their choosing to provide us with five years to prove ourselves may indicate some framework of values they follow. Despite some historical examples of humans acting as if power and wealth determine all, our visitors seem to adhere to a different standard."

There was some grumbling and a few guffaws. Another reporter rose. "So, are you defending their behavior? Like, maybe we deserve to be treated this way because of our history with the Native Americans and the African slave market?"

Derek realized he had made an error and responded quickly.

"I apologize, and I appreciate your having called it to my attention so quickly. Our history we can debate another day, but today, we have to shape our future response to our visitors.

"But you illustrate another issue we must face. What we are going to have to do over the next several years is to learn not to box people in with stereotypes but to listen deeply to each other. Each of us is worthy of being heard, even when we are wrong, so we know that we are of value as a human being."

"But how can we prove our worth if we don't know the criteria by which we are being measured?" asked another reporter.

"I think the answer is that we don't try to prove our worth to them. Rather, I think we try to demonstrate the best in us and trust the God who created us.

"If the stories are accurate about the early Christians being thrown to the lions, they didn't go into those coliseums to convince the crowd that they were worthy. They went to be worthy of the God who loved them."

Another reporter stood up. "So, are you saying this is a religious thing—that we must face our own lions?"

"No, and I think the fact that I'm a pastor is confusing what the mayor wanted to accomplish at this news conference. The churches, synagogues, and other religious communities will get together and discuss how our faith speaks to our value as human beings. You'll hear about what they propose later. But now, no matter what you believe or even if you believe, we are trying to decide how we want to respond to our visitors as citizens.

"They challenge us to demonstrate our worth as human beings. Do you think you are a higher life form than a pig or an eagle? If so, how do we build a community in Walnut Cove that makes that obvious to our visitors?

"Truth is, we don't know what they will do, but I'd rather face my lions with integrity and be comfortably pleased with how I lived my life, wouldn't you?"

Derek turned and welcomed the mayor to come to the mike.

CHAPTER 10
THE KINGDOM OF GOD AMONG US

Derek and Michal were responsible for drawing the churches together and seeking their response. Using the clergy council of the city, Michal and Derek arranged for five representative councils of religious leaders from across the city. They composed a letter to as many leaders as possible. The letter was shared with members of the council.

Their essential message was this: "In response to the Saucer message, we wish to convene several (at least five) meetings of representative religious leaders to identify a variety of possible responses to what appears to be their challenge."

"First, it is vital that we affirm our belief that God is Lord of history and seek to reassure our people that though this tragic reality has shaken our lives, we can continue to turn to God guided by spiritual leaders like yourselves. Even though we may have differing opinions, we are all charged with offering spiritual leadership.

"Second, we would like to behave towards our neighbors in a manner that the Saucer people can see the value we see in each other.

"Mostly, we want to build an awareness of the value we

witness in our neighbors who live near or far away.

"We would ask that you each convene in one of the five designated locations in the city. At your meeting, we hope each group can come to a consensus about what they hope our Saucer Visitors will see that reflects the value we see in each other.

"During this crisis, we suggest that all of us consider ways to demonstrate these basic beliefs in behavior that will contribute to the salvation of humanity."

"Do you think that they will believe us?" asked Kara.

"Not everyone," said Michal, "but we hope that, with a sufficient number, we can begin to counter the toxic poison of division as God in Christ would want us to do anyway."

"Do you think that a real church transformation might emerge out of this tragedy?" Helen asked.

"Ironic, isn't it? I don't believe God brought the Saucer people here to save us, but like some Bible stories, God often transforms tragedy into hope. As the old Gospel hymn says: 'We've a story to tell' (not only to the nations but also to the planets." And in the process, maybe we will deepen the spiritual life of our churches as well," said Derek.

"You know, I've prayed that prayer about the Kingdom coming on earth as it is in heaven about a zillion times, but I don't think I've ever stopped to think about what that would really look like," said Helen.

Everyone paused. They looked away as if they were embarrassed. Then Kara spoke up. "You aren't alone, Helen. I'll bet that if you put one thousand people together and asked that question, less than a hundred would raise their hands."

Jess chuckled. "And probably ten of them would be lying."

"OK, here's an idea. Why don't each of us ask at least ten other people what they think our city would look like if God's kingdom came and God's will was done in Walnut Cove," said Kara.

"That would be fun and maybe enlightening, but what do we think the answer would be?" said Derek as he rose to get a fresh cup of coffee.

"If God's will were being done, the saucer people would land and be both friendly and full of technological wisdom that could improve our lives," said Antonio.

"Do you think their presence can be both for our benefit and for theirs?" asked Kara.

"Sorry, I was being selfish," said Antonio.

"I didn't say that, but when was the last time we asked what they needed? According to Derek, they have travelled zillions of miles trying to find places where they might provide a decent home for people other than themselves."

"Dang, Kara, I hate it when you make sense, and I have to change my thinking."

"Wow, this is getting deep. What is one of the central truths of knowing God loves us?"

"I don't know how literal we should take the Scriptures, but our Scriptures say that 'God so loved the world that he gave his only begotten son.'"

"In a literal sense, God is pretty distant from us, and Jesus, though born here on earth, had to travel a long way to get here."

"So, are our visitors sent by God to visit and straighten us out?" asked Helen.

"This is all very confusing to me," said Kara. "Are you saying that God is the God of our visitors as well?"

"Derek, you are the only one who has communicated with them, and you are a preacher, for crying out loud," said Eric. "How do you answer that?"

"I don't answer all of that. It even gets more complicated when you combine Jesus and the cross. Did Jesus die for them, or did they have a different Messiah, or were they saved differently?

"This has shaken my faith as much as anyone. Last night I couldn't get the story of Jonah out of my mind."

"Ah, yes, the only sign you'll get is the sign of Jonah," said Kara. "That really helps clarify things. What are we supposed to do, find a belly of a whale to climb in?"

"Jonah didn't climb into the belly of a whale," said Derek. "In fact, he tried to do the opposite. Instead of doing what

God asked, he literally ran the other way. But then came a turning point."

"What do you mean?" asked Kara.

"That was always a favorite story when I was a child. Jonah tried to run away, but when a storm threatened everyone else's lives, he was willing to sacrifice himself for their sake just as Jesus would later on the cross."

"So, are we supposed to sacrifice ourselves for the sake of our visitors, or for the people on the earth, or what?"

"First," said Derek, "remember I'm the one who brought up the story. It may have nothing to do with our reality except to make us think in fresh ways."

"It's a rather confusing story. If I remember correctly, "said Eleanor, "Jonah did go to Nineveh, and the people did repent. That ticked Jonah off more than his original assignment."

"You are right," said Derek. "God's final words to Jonah were that his vision was always too small. He was disgusted when God caused the sun and wind to destroy a plant that had comforted Jonah, but he could dismiss the Ninevites without pity."

"So, are you suggesting that our vision may also be too small and that we need to respond to our new neighbors with compassion and respect as well? To use another Biblical story," said Brooke, "like the wise men of old, they have come a long distance, across a universe, in pursuit of a new truth."

“The question is can we bear the truth that they will recognize? If I remember correctly, those earlier wisemen didn’t exactly meet with an eager audience. Maybe the real question is can we recognize the truth if they point to it?”

“This is getting scary, dude,” said Erik.

“We began by saying that maybe we need to rethink the church. I’m not sure our people will be eager to respond to this new understanding of the church, “said Eleanor.

“Like the early church, some will, and some won’t. But our task is to at least give them a choice.”

“Maybe I need to reconsider that question about being called by God. God has some weird reasons and expectations in issuing a call.”

CHAPTER 11
A SECOND ASSEMBLY OF CHURCHES

This time Derek and Michal sent invitations to the clergy and religious leaders of the city, asking them to come to an emergency meeting at the Glory to God assembly hall on 42 Street. It had the largest assembly hall among churches in the city and, under the circumstances, was willing to waive the rental fee.

Two days later, over one hundred clergy began to arrive at the Assembly Hall. "It's amazing," said one cynical newscaster, "how a visit from some aliens from another planet can cause our pastors who are constantly preaching about love to at least demonstrate they can be in the same room together."

At about 8:45, Derek, Michal, an Orthodox Priest, a Bishop from the Catholic church, and several Protestant leaders, a Jewish Rabbi, and an Imam from a Muslim community ascended the steps prepared to convene the gathering of the religious leadership of the city. They had decided that the mayor would convene them as a neutral spokesperson for the city.

To facilitate their exchange, the clergy were asked to sit at tables of eight. Each table had small cards with numbers one through nine and a small battery-powered mike.

Eleanor stepped before the mike and called them together. “I’ve spoken before a lot of groups during my life as a politician. I’ve never spoken to such a gathering of religious leaders before. It’s a little intimidating.”

A voice came out of the audience. “Relax. We are really pretty nice when you get to know us.”

Eleanor acknowledged the comment and proceeded, “I would say before we begin that there has never been a more important gathering in this city, and I urge you, the spiritual leaders in this city, to provide spiritual guidance and restore a sense of hope to our city.”

We will open with a moment of silence, respecting that there is a great diversity among us, even about how we pray.”

There was an embarrassed chuckle that swept over the crowd.

The cameraman who was filming the event turned toward his assistant. “Make sure that you film this part. It may be just the miracle of so many preachers being silent, but” he paused and even swallowed, “just maybe the Spirit will move, and God’s spirit will touch us. We could use a miracle about now.”

They waited for a few minutes, and then Eleanor said, “Amen.”

When they had raised their heads to look at her, she simply said: “I wish you luck. As one exhausted and frightened member of one of your churches, I pray for you, desperately hope for your prayers, and invite your cooperation with the city over the next weeks, months, and maybe even years. Again, I say Thank you."

With that, Eleanor left the stage to a polite applause and stood off stage.

Derek approached the mike. "For reasons I cannot understand, I am the only person I know who has received direct communication from our visitors. Their message was simple and direct: "They are searching for a planet that they can colonize with populations from another planet."

"How do we know that isn't a hoax broadcast that was sent to confuse us?" shouted one pastor from a table close to the stage.

"Honestly, David," Michal recognized the speaker, "We don't know. We know that the Saucers hover over our city and have enveloped us in an impenetrable bubble, but that is about all we know."

"And," said Derek, "we know that they seem to have incredible technology that could handle our missile attempt as if they were just swatting at flies. I understand your skepticism, but as long as what we do benefits and doesn't degrade our population, I'm not sure what we have to lose."

Another man stood up further back in the room. He had spotted the mike at his table and decided to use it. "We can view everything with a little skepticism, but doing nothing is like surrendering before the battle begins. I'd like to hear a little more about what Derek heard that day."

One could almost feel the room lean forward as Derek lifted his mike.

"Here is where it gets a little strange. Their message seemed to suggest that because there are only a limited number of planets that can sustain living creatures, their universal council, whatever that is, determined that these planets should be parceled out to those who were most worthy."

Another man popped up from the audience with a mic in his hand. "What standard are they using to determine a population's measure of worth?"

"They didn't say what their criteria were. They only said that they would observe us for a period of five Earth years to determine our worth. We have about four left. If we are found to be worthy, they will leave us alone and look for another planet. If not, they will begin the process of replacement of one population for the other."

One of the city's more liberal clergy guffawed and said, "I guess that is more than we gave the Indigenous population in this country or how we treated the Africans we brought over to do our work."

Michal approached the mike. "You are all sitting at tables that hold eight. We are asking that you spend the next 45 minutes to an hour trying to define some basic principles that, if they were reflected in our relationships, would show our value and worth both as individuals and as a community."

"At the end of that time," added Derek, "we will gather your table reports and see if Christians can at least agree on the basic principles of how we should live."

Another man in the crowd immediately grabbed the mike and stood up.

"I don't need no forty-five minutes. "And I don't need no Saucer people," his voice was filled with disdain, "to tell me how I should live. My Savior is Jesus Christ, my Lord and Savior. He will determine when I die and where I will go after I die. To think otherwise is pure blasphemy."

There was some applause as he sat down.

Derek reached for the mike. He tried to speak calmly. "Let me build on what Terry just said. We don't know what our visitors want, but at some level or another, Christians and Muslims have affirmed much of what Jesus taught. Even our Jewish friends have affirmed the basic message of justice and compassion that Jesus proclaimed. "Derek paused and looked over the gathering of clergy, "while we may differ on some parts of that, I doubt if there are many here who would claim to perfectly follow Jesus' commands."

Bishop Ferguson, who had accompanied them onto the stage, reached out for the mike. "I come from a different tradition than most of you, but our common prayer that our Lord taught us is the center of our shared faith. Our task is to seek to live as if God's kingdom has come and God's will is being done. That demonstrates our worth, regardless of what our visitors think."

Derek added, "I believe that the city is very interested in supporting us in your efforts, as I hope you are in theirs.

"If the gentleman who just spoke wants to repeat his position in his small group, that is appropriate, but we are now going to take the time to allow others to speak as well."

"Remember, we don't know what the Saucer people think gives us value as humans, so what we can do as churches reflect the values that Jesus gave us. As a way to begin, I have sheets for each of you that contain the Beatitudes that Jesus spoke as recorded in Matthew 5:1 -12 as well as a summary copy of Paul's advice in Romans 12. Of course, you can use other Scriptures or traditions, but this can at least be a beginning.

"We'll be wandering around if any of you need help, but mainly, I'd like to see you working with your table grouping," added Michal.

"We'll check in with you in about an hour to see your progress.

"What we would like for you to do is describe how you seek to embody one of those principles in your life as a church or whatever religious community you participate in. For example, if you chose Blessed are the Merciful, you might identify a couple of categories of members who could benefit from a church that demonstrated mercy as part of living the Kingdom. You might even suggest how the church can be merciful to those constant complainers among our members. How can the church be merciful to the more impoverished among members? There are lots of options. Try to reduce it to one or two and trust that others will pick up what you didn't choose."

Derek leaned into the mike. "After we have heard those reports, we will shift our focus to society and identify a couple of institutions that could benefit from a strong expression of compassion and appreciation to their constituents. One example might be how you can focus mercy on those incarcerated or those failing in school.

"We have some ideas about how to proceed from there, but, as we are going to suggest with the membership of our churches, we want to begin with what you already believe."

You could hear the intense conversation around the tables for the next fifty-five minutes. Sometimes there were brief arguments, but it only required someone to point to the ceiling, indicating the presence of the Saucers, to remind them that they had to set aside some differences.

Ralph brought Derek and Michal a cup of black coffee and cookies. "I'll admit I appreciated that the two of you were helping organize this, and I am pleased that I could offer the facilities, but I'm afraid that I was skeptical that anything could result from this except a lot of self-promotion. Looking at the intensity of the conversations, I'm beginning to pray for a miracle and almost believing that God might provide one.

As Derek mentioned early on, I don't believe that God arranged for the Saucers to teach us a lesson, but I do hope God can use this experience to help us understand our faith more deeply," said another clergy standing there.

At the end of the time set aside, Derek said, "Let's turn on the projection screens and begin to find out what has been happening. You have some of your people taking notes as we proceed, right?"

Derek spoke into the mike. "Let's reconvene. This is not going to be easy, but for the sake of the citizens of our city, I hope and pray that we can begin, and I emphasize begin, to re-imagine what both our religious communities and our city would look like if we devoted ourselves to live and witness to God's kingdom being lived in this city."

Ralph added, "We are going to ask each table to report in short sentences the major conclusions they reached on how we should relate and make Christ's presence felt in the institutions of our city."

"There are twelve tables, and we will record what you report, but we ask you also to keep your notes for further use as we proceed. Let's begin with Table #1.

Each table took their turn reporting their conversations for the next hour.

They struggled with the Beatitudes.

"What if," a table spokesperson said, "from this day forward, we Christians seek to 'Love one another with mutual affection and outdo one another in showing honor to everyone.' That way, we will show our Saucer friends that, though we are not sure of their criteria, we value each other."

"Let's move to Table 2," Michal said as a scribe wrote out what had been shared.

"There are lots of people who are struggling to survive in this hostile atmosphere. Maybe it's time for our churches to unite in 'extending hope to strangers and blessing even those who persecute us. It's time to rejoice with those who are joyful and weep with those who are weeping.' That's surely what God wants us to do now."

And so, it continued as each table tried to express the behavior they believed would demonstrate the value of their community.

The host pastor, Ralph, said, "Let me make a suggestion. Let's return to our respective churches, report on what we have shared, and seek to live a couple of these values out concerning each other and maybe three or four other religious communities as well.

“We’ll meet again in four days and share what we have experienced.”

“And what if we fail miserably? Will the Saucer people begin to pluck us up and toss us away?” said a woman from Table number 6?”

“I don’t know, Mary, but at least we will have tried with new energy to live out the faith we proclaim,” said Ben from a table nearby.

As the assembly began to dissipate, several clergy approached those on the stage and thanked them for this effort.

CHAPTER 12
FRESH CITY THINKING

Jess invited Antonio and Kara to meet him for drinks at the Zimmer Lounge on Arizona Street. He had arrived early to secure a quiet corner.

Rick, his favorite bar master, greeted him and ushered him towards the reserved corner. "I've got you set up in Pelican Corner, Mr. Franklin. Should be no problem with conversation over there."

Jess looked around the richly decorated lounge. The thick carpet and sound-defeating banners on several walls had always encouraged businesspeople to use the lounge for informal business conversations.

"Sorry I haven't been around much lately, Rick. Looks like lots of people are being cautious these days."

"You're part of the Mayor's Council, aren't you, Mr. Franklin? Can't they figure out some way to handle this? It's spooky watching those Saucers but not hearing any communication."

"We're working on it, Rick. That's what Kara and Antonio are meeting me to do. What would you do to demonstrate our worth and value as a city?"

"I'm in the hospitality business, Mr. Franklin. People come here all stressed out and anxious. I help them get back in touch with their inner joy."

He chuckled and continued. "A good drink and some delicious snacks can help lower the pressure and bring back some of the joy."

"Here come my guests. Let's test out that theory. I'll start with a double Vodka Martini. Not sure what they want to drink."

Rick quickly ushered them to their table and took their drink orders. "We have some burgundy splashed chicken wings for a snack. How does that sound?"

"Bring it on," said Antonio. "I've given up watching my weight. What's the point?"

Kara smiled and said, "I'm not quite that wild at this moment. Why not bring me some crackers with some spicy cheese?"

Jess nodded. "I'll go with Kara's choice. However, I watched her with the hot sauce. Make mine a little milder."

Rick smiled. Tell you what. Mr. Franklin mentioned the topic of your conversation. Let me offer the first drink and snack on the house."

"All right, maybe with some good snacks and a drink, we will come up with some creative ideas yet," said Antonio.

Rick headed back to his bar, and Jess turned towards his

guests. "Funny how important little things can be. Rick just offered us both a warm greeting and a free snack. How do those two small things make you feel right now?"

"I'm looking forward to the snack," said Antonio, "and I feel like Rick cares for us, maybe even likes us as customers."

"So, you would trust him," said Jess.

"What's your point?" Kara asked.

"In one way, what he did was so simple," said Jess, "and yet it has a powerful impact. How do we do that for the rest of our citizens?"

"When I came to this country, I immediately had two experiences that stuck with me ten years later. The first was an interview--it felt like a grilling by an immigration agent. I know he was just doing his job, but I felt like he was suspicious, and his big purpose was to catch me in some mistake so he could reject my application.

"Not long afterward, my host showed up with a bouquet and a big smile. At that point, if she asked me to polish her boots, I would have done it gladly."

"So, our task is to help our citizens not get so caught up in the drama of events that they forget to affirm the positive," said Antonio.

"We can't do that personally for each citizen, but we can show them how to do that for each other," said Jess.

"It's still summertime; why don't we have a series of 'We

love our neighbors' festivals around the city and introduce the skill of in-depth listening?" asked Antonio. "We could design them in fun ways while addressing the Saucer issue at the same time."

"If we could do that in a way that would reduce the fear and anxiety of their presence, that might have real value. The problem is that we can't communicate with the saucers."

"Yet they seem to be very aware of us. What if we explained that to our citizens and invited them to design what they wanted the Saucer people to hear? At least they would feel they are beginning to communicate, even if it is just one way," said Antonio.

"Let me build on that," said Kara. "The question they posed for us is whether we have value and worth to justify continuing to populate this planet. Maybe our first two-way communication is to answer that question. Let's get together, have fun, build community, and affirm our worth."

"I think that has possibilities," said Jess. "But I don't think I'd stop there. Let's build the festivals around where people can buy food—restaurants, corner stores, fast food places, etc. Having a little food will help lift the spirits of those who gather, and the economy will benefit at the same time."

"Why don't we build in some challenges during the event? We can give a small prize to the group that brings the best idea about how to love their neighbor. It emphasizes our theme, and someone might come up with some unique ideas."

"And, with what we just witnessed with Rick and his effect on us, let's also bring ideas of the best ways to welcome and affirm a stranger in our crowd."

"The mayor introduced a great idea soon after this all started," said Antonio. "Every evening at six, someone from the administration comes on our local television with an update on what is happening. That would be a perfect opportunity to build interest in our event."

"Let's start with getting the schools and recreation centers involved by letting them pick the location for the events. We can advertise them at the schools and during our six o'clock broadcast. The more people we involve, the better off we are," said Antonio.

"Here's an idea. Let's separate each group according to such things as gender, age blocks, and health conditions. We ask them the same question and see how their responses indicate the group they are in. How do the women answer versus the men, the young versus the old, the healthy versus the disabled, etc.? Then during our celebrations, we can reveal different winners and invite the audience to celebrate the best ones. With our new technology, we can broadcast our winners all at the same time around the city. That will enhance the mood of the city."

They continued to talk for another hour, each sparking off

the other and growing as a group in enthusiasm.

"OK," said Jess. "I think that will wrap it up for now. I'll start working on more details about the gatherings, and we will meet again next week. Same place and time."

"Why didn't we have these saucer people around at the beginning," said Rick. "These are some pretty good ideas."

"I won't mention the obvious," said Antonio, "but loving your neighbor is hardly new."

CHAPTER 13
HOW DO YOU EDUCATE FOR A LIMITED FUTURE

As some form of life's routines began to re-establish themselves, the issue of the school came up. If parents were going to continue to work, what would they do with the children? The schools, teachers, and Board of Education also raised questions about what they would teach. In the most general sense, it was always assumed that, in some manner or other, the purpose of education was to prepare students for the future. But what if there was the possibility that there was no future? What should you teach then?

Edward O'Brien, head of the city's teachers' union, became a powerful spokesperson for raising that key issue. "How do we prepare our children for the future if no one is sure there will be a future? We go into the classroom and try to teach physics, finances, and world history, and our students just stare at us, if they attend at all. Their attitude is, 'If there are only a couple of years left, why bother?' What is the value of education if there is no future?"

After debating this for a couple of weeks, Ted Killinger, another member of the teachers' union, finally brought a report to a joint meeting of the school board and the Teachers

Union. "Our alien visitors in the Saucers have challenged us to re-evaluate the purpose of our public education system as a whole. As one of my students said the other day, 'If I only have a couple of years left, I'd rather go swimming or hang out at the Flying Eagle to listen to music and eat some good food.'"

"As you know, we represent some teachers who, a couple of weeks ago, set aside our normal classes and started asking a bunch of our students if our future is short, what we would like to know more about in our short future. Their answers were very helpful. I've asked one of those students to speak to you about this. Her name is Karen Bellinger."

Karen stood up. From the back of the room, a chair scraped, and a sturdy woman of about five-foot began to advance towards the front of the room. A cane helped her steady an apparently injured ankle. She was clearly nervous, but there was a look of determination on her face as she spoke.

She held the council with a steady gaze and began to speak. "The first thing we thought about is we really don't know what the saucerites are going to do, so we need to plan how to support each other and be a community regardless of what takes place."

"That's what we are trying to do," said a member of the Teacher's Board.

"I know that," said Karen, "but you are all doing that in

secret. We don't even know who will be left if the saucerites take some direct action. When Mr. Killenger asked us what we wanted to learn, many of us thought the most important skill we could learn was thinking together when everything seemed to be falling apart. Any idiot can figure out how to fight, argue, shout, and scream. But how do you think together so that you are getting the best gifts from everyone?"

"And does Mr. Killinger know how to teach you that?" asked another school board member.

"It seems to me," said the mayor, sitting in on the meeting, "that there couldn't be a more important focus for our schools over the next several years. If this city learned how to think and listen clearly to each other during our isolation, we'd have a major gift to offer our world and our guests in the saucers."

"So, what are you proposing, Mr. Killinger?"

"I'm not sure, other than we need to learn the skill to listen to each other and to gain the confidence to not be threatened when someone disagrees with us."

"May I say something more?" asked Kara.

"Of course; what is it?"

"If, as Reverend Mansfield reported, the saucerites are trying to determine how valuable we are, shouldn't some of our efforts be at believing that the other person is valuable and has something to say? We only learn that if we learn to listen."

"You are a very mature young lady, Kara," said Sally, a

teacher at the meeting. "But you don't have the same life experience that most of us here have."

"But we can learn if we are given the opportunity. Why don't you give each school a problem you think we might face? We'll try to come up with some solutions. They won't all be good, but the process will help us prepare for what might happen in our future."

"It can't hurt, and we could use some fresh thinking. Who knows what these saurcerites will come up with. — I like the name saurcerites, by the way," said Edward O'Brian.

"We can let the city know which schools are working on which problems and encourage school gatherings to share their work," said Sally. "This could be both exciting and fun."

"Sounds pretty idealistic to me," said Tim. "Do you really think some juvenile can come up with solutions to this crisis?"

"No, I don't," said Jess, "but it will be interesting to see the effect of the city pulling together. I'm sure many of you know the Bible better than me, but didn't Jesus suggest that children were pretty important to the advance of the kingdom?"

"I know we must think this through more thoroughly, "said the mayor. "If you were to identify up to ten areas of improvement we will face in the years leading up to our deadline, what would you suggest they will be? — Anyone?"

"I'd say housing is a big one. For a city to be healthy, we need to solve the problem of homelessness. I know that some people will be more prosperous than others, but we'd solve a lot of problems if everyone had a decent place to live," said Kara.

That's an interesting challenge, Kara. If we ask these young people to help respond to the saucer challenge to prove our worth, I would add another one. My area is health care. What would these young people suggest our society could do to demonstrate the value of an individual's health?"

"I think this is wonderful," said Ted. "It will be a little scary for some teachers, but what you are saying is that the best education includes taking the students seriously and helping them listen to each other."

"Gee, maybe if our students learned to listen to each other and solve problems as a team, they might pass that talent on to the adults," said Sally.

"With all this taking place in our city, don't you wonder what the Saucerites are...?"

He paused and nodded at Kara. "Don't you wonder what they are thinking?"

Eleanor interrupted. "I don't know what they are thinking, but the more I listen to people trying to work this out, the more I am proud to be mayor of this city."

CHAPTER 14
MONEY DIVIDES

Kara Beeman drummed her fingers on the table as she awaited her lunch companions. She was nervous but rather excited. When the mayor asked her to convene the justice task force, she had no idea where this could go. For the last fifteen years, while she taught English at the state university, she also enjoyed volunteering to serve on several justice task forces in various parts of Walnut Cove but never felt they accomplished very much.

Now, suddenly, she had the opportunity to change the world—or at least the part in which she lived. Derek had helpfully divided life into seven parts, and the mayor had assigned Kara, a businesswoman from India, the area of the courts and justice. A local banker and Eric had also been asked to be put on the task force to brainstorm possibilities.

And then last night happened. She was sitting watching a silly TV program alone when the phone rang. The caller announced himself. "Kara, my name is Carlton Griffin. I'm your cousin, the son of your Aunt Flora."

"Oh, yeah, I remember you. Except, the last I heard, you were in our local prison with a fifteen-year sentence for graft and embezzlement in a local financial institution."

"I'm afraid your memory is very accurate. I screwed up big time and am now a resident of the Walnut Cove prison."

"Are you calling from the prison?"

"Yep, I still have twelve years to serve. I hope, however, that I have grown up and gotten a little smarter in the process. It may seem strange, but this criminal cousin of yours has been thinking, and I have an idea."

"Uh, what's that?" Kara asked.

As I understand from the newspaper, you are on the mayor's task force trying to figure out how our city responds to this Saucer mystery."

"That's true, Carlton, but what does that have to do with your time in prison?" Kara was skeptical but set her drink down and picked up a tablet and pen.

"Is it true," Carlton asked, "that our city residents have about three years left to prove their worth?"

"That's accurate, but we don't know what will happen then."

"Well, I have about twelve years, and I was wondering if I could use the next three to help you and the city and perhaps lessen my sentence in the process."

"I'm not sure I understand."

Carlton cleared his throat. "As I said, I have twelve years left, and the city has only about three. What if I can offer you and your task force a way to demonstrate our value as humans?"

"I'm listening," said Kara.

"I read somewhere that the mayor's task force is considering renaming our prison and again calling it a reformatory. Prisons warehouse people and make them largely useless. Reformatories are supposed to prepare them for the future."

"The laws that changed reformatories is a statewide law. I'm not sure we have time to change that, even if you had a miraculous medicine to offer."

"Wait, hear me out. We are an isolated city cut off from the world, and it doesn't look like that will end soon. Who would stop us if the council suddenly tried to make big changes? And, if we are right, then a small group of people could literally change the world."

"What type of changes are you thinking about?" The thought of changing some of the practices of our major institutions intrigued Kara. She quickly changed from daydreaming to listening carefully.

"Do you know much about Alcoholics Anonymous, Ms. Beeman?"

"Not a lot, and why don't you call me Kara? We are family, after all."

Carlton chuckled, but Kara also felt him relax a bit.

'In AA, the first thing you have to do is take ownership of your past behavior. Something like, 'My name is Carlton

Griffin, and I am an alcoholic.'

Now it was time for Kara to laugh. "I'm sure you realize that your reputation extends far beyond alcoholism."

Carlton continued. "Wait, let me say it for you. 'My name is Carlton Griffin. I'm a greedy, tech-wise, fairly intelligent but self-centered, s.o.b."

Kara smiled and nodded. "You left out family hating and womanizing."

"The list does get fairly long, but after you have owned all of your shortcomings in AA, the next part is fairly important, I think. You have to also admit that you can't change for the better by yourself. That to really change, you need both human and divine support."

"I don't know a lot about AA, but that all makes sense. What does that have to do with us?"

"I need that help, Kara, but I also have some gifts that the city needs."

"Go on."

"As you are well aware, an area where the city has its greatest difficulty is in the area of finances. That happens to be an area in which I have some expertise."

"It's certainly an area where we are having difficulties. No institution in the city can pay salaries, and people have to be very selective about using their cash. Even then, there is no guarantee the other person will attribute value to the piece of paper we use."

"What happens if the city develops its own financial system? Your disgraced relative was in prison for a scheme using Crypto Currency. If the council would approve me, I, and some friends, could set up our own city system of Crypto Currency. It would be a way of getting our economy running again in the city.

"In the process, Kara, I could be one of your first reformed citizens and regain my dignity simultaneously."

"Carlton, that is an intriguing idea. Of course, I'd have to explore it with the Council, but, as so happens, they meet tomorrow morning. I can't make any promises, but you will hear back from me."

"I've been waiting several years; another few days won't hurt. By the way, if they buy my idea, several financial figures will want to feed at the same trough. Make sure that you pick wisely."

Kara hung up the phone and had a sense of excitement she hadn't felt for quite a while. Her first step was to get in touch with Mike Berrigan. Mike was a sharp banker who had a mind of his own. He was modestly conservative but not afraid to take some chances. His comments in the recent Council meetings indicated that he was struggling to develop a plan.

"Alexa, call Mike Berrigan at his office."

"Calling Mike Berrigan at his office," Alexa announced and

proceeded to make the call.

The call was answered four rings later: “This is Mike Berrigan’s office. To whom am I speaking?”

“Gail, this is Kara Beeman. Is Mike in and available? I have some information that I think will interest him.”

“I hope it’s good news. He could use a lift to his spirits, and frankly, so could I. It’s rather creepy around here since all the ATM and business windows were closed.”

“Thanks, Gail. If it turns out good, you will be among the first ones to know.”

Kara could picture Gail punching the intercom and announcing Kara’s presence on the phone.

“Kara,” Mike said. “Good to hear from you. What’s up?”

“I just heard from a resident of our newly named reformatory. This one happens to be a cousin, son of my Uncle Harry. He has an idea I think is worth exploring before we bring it to the council.”

“A family member, huh? That alone catches my interest. This has to do with finances, I assume.”

“It does. Are you sitting down, and your coffee is in a solid place on your desk?”

“Now you have my attention. Just a second.”

Kara heard Mike’s voice speaking out through his intercom. “Gail, hold my calls for the next half-hour or so. I’ll let you know when Kara and I are through.” He returned the phone.

"OK, Kara, tell me about your cousin."

"I can tell you more later, but you need to know this much up front. His major was in economics; before he got in trouble, he worked in the financial field. From what I heard from his mother, he really had a gift for finances and economics, but he also had some impulse control issues."

"And then," Mike said, "I'm guessing he got bored and decided to get creative with the numbers."

"Something like that. I don't know all the details, but he got involved with Crypto Currency."

Kara heard a slight groan on the line, but Mike quickly came back to her. "I don't know how much you know about that idea, but it is basically a way around our currency system. What is your cousin suggesting?

"If it holds any promise, I'd want you to talk with him. Both of you would know the questions and pitfalls to discuss, but basically, I heard him saying that he thinks that our city could develop a system within our bubble that we would control but would help commerce take place."

Kara could hear Mike breathing heavily over the phone.

"You know, Kara, I'd have to think this through, but as much as I'm surprised to hear me say this, I think your cousin might have an idea worth exploring."

"Interesting. Well, he's done a lot of thinking about this. Do you think it might be worth sitting down with him and pushing it around?"

"Let me call a couple of close friends and set up a meeting. I'm assuming that since he's in prison, we could pull him out almost any time we wanted. I'll get back to you within the hour."

Thanks, Mike. I'll wait for your call. You know the university is not too far from the prison, and I could easily set aside a room if it would help."

"I'll let you know. Thanks."

The line went dead. Kara felt a slight shiver. Could this be significant, she wondered.

Within an hour, Mike called back. "OK, I've got some excitement on my end. Why don't you see if you can get a room set up for tomorrow afternoon? Text me back, and we'll meet at the university with your cousin, let's say at three in the afternoon. How does that sound?

"Actually, it sounds rather exciting. I'll be back with the room arrangements in less than a half hour. Thanks, Mike; talk to you soon."

Kara called the University President's office and immediately arranged for a conference room in the southwest corner of the campus. There was a parking lot near the building and a convenient Starbucks on the first floor.

She then arranged with the warden to have Carlton Griffin delivered the next day at 2 p.m. Eric Johnson and the youth she had recently met, Karen Beeman, completed her task force. She also invited Michal Talbert to bring a faith perspective on this weird situation.

Mike Berrigan invited Antonio Beard to complete his side.

Once she had confirmed all the participants, she contacted the prison to reconfirm the details of his release for the meeting. She had a couple of easels and plenty of paper and pens delivered to the room. Next, she called Starbucks and arranged for extra coffee and donuts.

They all arrived by three in the afternoon.

Carlton gave a brief background and then shared his idea with the task force. "I don't have to tell you what a financial mess we are experiencing. I shared with Aunt Kara that I think we can take advantage of our situation and maybe even benefit from it."

"I can tell you for sure that there are roughly one-hundred banks that are still open in this city, and most of them are operating on bare fumes," said Jess. "We could use some good news."

"Give me an example of what they can and can't do at this moment," said Kara.

"As you know, we have no access to funds outside the city, so in addition to peoples' lock boxes, we are stuck with a minimal amount of cash that is trucked back and forth among the banks, which is a nightmare."

“So, what if we didn’t use cash,” asked Carlton, “and used our own version of Cryptro currency to facilitate our exchanges?”

“That’s fake money if you ask me,” said Eric. “They don’t use money, they just…(He paused, as everyone looked at him.) “. . .You know,” he said, “we live in a contained city. Bank robberies have tanked because there is no place to run. Loan sharks don’t have any cash to work with. The rich are better off than most, but they were accustomed to working with texts and faxes to move money that isn’t available now.

Are you suggesting that we create our own system of exchange?”

“With the city self-contained, and both cash and credit cards of little use, we might want to consider going further than that.”

“What do you mean?” asked Kara.

“Think about what wealth in its various versions has done to humanity in our history. Since we are demonstrating our self-worth, might we want to explore another way of financial and wealth exchange that builds people up rather than separates and divides them?”

“Give me an example of how it could be any different,” said Mike.

“I’ve been thinking about this while I sat in prison,” said Carlton. “It’s not always great food, but to quote the Bible, each day we are given that day our daily bread. That's one thing we didn't have to fight over."

"So, crime can be reduced in the city because everyone has enough to eat?" said Eric.

"Yes, and we can also focus on forgiveness and reward and celebrate those who use their gifts to build others up rather than tear them down. What happens if each week we recognize those banks and investment corporations that are especially nice to another person, especially a needy one? They can even be rewarded in some way."

"So, explain this to me again. How will this bank thing work?" asked Jess. "What will my bank people be doing?"

"Sounds like they will be helping each other make connections to assist in needs and joys. Someone comes in and says, 'I need money to make an addition to my house.'"

"The banker both seeks to match a builder with that person and tries to identify how that homeowner can return the favor. Both of them have enough to eat. They just need to find out how they can please and build each other up."

"On the one hand," Kara said, "we are being wildly idealistic, and yet within the confines of our city, it might work."

"Why don't you work out the details of such an idea, and then we can bring it to council for review. We are discovering that our saucer crisis is urging us to step beyond what we assumed as reality and explore new ways of living our lives as a community."

CHAPTER 15
CELEBRATION OF THE MAYOR

Eleanor ended what felt like the thirtieth call that day. Why had she ever chosen to run for office as mayor of Walnut Cove? Of course, when she began her campaign, it was simply a nice city of two thousand citizens, and she thought being mayor would be a nice change from defending the innocent and prosecuting the guilty in courts. There were several projects that, if you had the political courage, might make life more pleasant. The recent change among several of the city's institutions, focusing on people rather than the bottom line, had a major institutional impact.

She felt a sharp pain in the back of her neck. At least it is in the neck and not in the chest, she thought. She looked forward to the massage her husband had arranged when she left the office.

She would say one thing about the crisis and its effect on her life. Before the Visitors came, her marriage had been moderately comfortable, if a little boring. The fear and uncertainty that had erupted across her city had been hard on many families, but in her case, it had brought her and her husband closer together than ever.

She giggled a little bit. In addition to having discovered all sorts of ways to support each other, they had also experienced some new forms of intimacy that were exciting.

Her intercom buzzed as her assistant reminded her that the now almost daily meeting of the City Council was her next, and hopefully last, commitment of her day. Then, she thought, as she rubbed her neck, I'll get that massage.

Antonio, her faithful clerk, met her as she exited the office. "Madam mayor, your devoted Council awaits your presence."

"And have you made arrangements in case some of our Visitors decide to grace us with their presence?" she asked.

"Fuck em," he said, shaking his head. "One thing I've admired in your response to this situation is that you have kept your focus on improving life in the city. If we survive this, our city will be one city as close to Paradise here on Earth as there ever will be.

"It's ironic, isn't it?" she said. "They came to threaten and even replace us, but they've caused us to both develop a new respect for each other and cooperate in a way that brings out the best in a variety of people who previously wouldn't even speak to each other."

As they entered the boardroom, the seven members of the City Council rose with a burst of applause. "Madam mayor," said Kara, "pardon my language, but in my humble opinion, you look like shit."

"And recognizing that unique form of beauty and knowing that it is critical to occasionally experience some interruption of the stress that you are under, we have arranged for a brief interruption of our meeting. May I present to you "Miss Sonia Wallace from San Francisco? Your husband tells us she is one of your favorite singers, and she has agreed to sing two songs to express our gratitude."

Antonio brought forth a comfortable chair while announcing, "It is the council's unanimous vote that you are to sit here and say absolutely nothing until Sonia has finished."

Sonia took a seat in front of her and began to strum her guitar. "This is an old song, but it still speaks the truth," she said. With that, she began to sing Bob Dylan's Blowing in the Wind. Eleanor held it together until Sonia began to sing the third verse.

Yes, and how many times must a man look up
Before he can see the sky?
Yes, and how many ears must one man have
Before he can hear people cry?
Yes, and how many deaths will it take till he knows
That too many people have died?

Eleanor wept and was speechless as her council surrounded her with a loving hug. Then Eric spoke up. "You know, I'm not much of a churchgoer, but my fiancée, a person of faith, suggested that we ask Sonia to sing one more song for you. We've asked Sonia to sing a hymn from your church songbook. It's called O For a World, and as I looked at it, I realized that it expresses much of what you have promoted in your effort to prove that we are worthy of living on this planet.

Sonia will sing all five verses," said Antonio, "but I've printed out copies of verses one and three for particular emphasis.

1. Oh, for a world where everyone respects each other's ways, where love is lived, and all is done with justice and with praise.

3. We welcome one world family and struggle with each choice that opens us to unity and gives our vision voice.

When Sonia was finished, Eleanor sat there speechless. Sonia rose. "As horrible as the past couple of years have been, I'm honored that I happened to be in the city to visit my cousin when everything shut down. Madam Mayor, I don't know what is happening out in the larger world. Like everyone else, I don't know what the future holds or even if we have a future. I do know that I am blessed to have been in this city under your leadership. Thank you."

With that, Sonia advanced, took Eleanor in her arms, and hugged her.

Eleanor took a deep breath. She looked at her Council, who were still standing and grinning. Many of them looked exhausted by the events of the last couple of years, but they also experienced the healing power of having participated in a community act of love, and they were feeling some renewed energy.

When Sonia had departed, Eleanor looked again at the seven people who had been her main support over this terrifying time. “I’m not sure I would be able to conduct this meeting after that. I love you all for what you have done.”

“I move that we adjourn until tomorrow evening,” said Jess, and there was a chorus of affirmation.

Slowly, with many hugs and voices of support, the room slowly emptied.

From around the corner, the voice of her husband spoke up. “I think it’s time I took you to get that celebratory massage we’ve been talking about.”

CHAPTER 16
CHILDREN PAINT PICTURES

Barrie walked out onto the porch to see what Felicity was doing. She was stretched out on a lounge chair near the edge of the pool. He could hear her talk to herself and even laugh at her own jokes. She was so intensely absorbed in what she was doing that she didn't even hear him approach her.

Since the saucers came, the last couple of years had been really strange. At first, everyone panicked. Schools closed, movie theaters and many recreation centers closed. At first, many people hid in their basements if they had one. There were lots of the end of the world prophets everywhere you looked.

Then, after six months, nothing had happened. The saucers just hovered over the city, but except for the missile incident, the saucer didn't even indicate that they knew people were down here. For a while, the city people would stare up at them, scream epitaphs, or utter pleas for mercy. A few even pulled out their guns and shot at them. But as wired as they were, life continued after a few months, and people adjusted.

As far as Barrie knew, the visitors only communicated once, and that was with his father. How cool was that? He was pretty popular with other kids for a while. But then, nothing happened, and people's attention span dwindled.

Their visual presence continued, and the bubble kept people from leaving the city. A couple of other times, a group decided to shoot a cannon or some other weapon at the ships. Without any emotional response, a burst of energy flashed like lightning and consumed the cannon, but that was it.

With the immediate fear gone, the whole city began to discuss and plan how they wanted to live in their isolated bubble.

The solitary message communicated by Barrie's father evolved in several forms. Several groups lost all boundaries of behavior. "If we only have five years left to live, what difference does it make if we want to drink all night, have sexual relations with our cousins, steal from a neighbor, or just lie around and stuff ourselves with unhealthy food?" they reasoned.

But then the churches started reminding people that the aliens had given them a choice. Their behavior would determine whether they survived or not. Like a disapproving parent, the saucers just hung around and observed. The city's residents made their own choices as to how they wanted to respond.

Barrie mentioned that to his father once. His mother spoke up before his father could respond. "It's sort of like it has always been. You choose your behavior, and how you act affects how you feel about yourself. If you act like a bully, you begin to feel like life belongs to the bullies. If you choose to be kind, generous, or loving, not only do people respond to you like a kind person, but you feel better about yourself. But the choice is yours."

"But the saucers are real, Momma," Felicity said. "Anytime they want to, they can send a lightning bolt and consume us."

"But they haven't, have they?" said Derek. "I wonder how bad or how good we have to get before they choose to respond?"

"They better get out of here before I get married," said Felicity. "I want everyone to feel happy at my wedding."

"Boy, they had better hurry up," said Derek. "Have you any particular boy picked out?"

"No, Daddy, I've got to become a famous artist first so that lots of handsome men will want to meet me."

Barrie chuckled at the memory and turned back towards his sister. "What are you doing, Felicity?"

"I'm painting pictures of our neighbors up there."

"No one has ever seen them. How can you paint them?"

"If they won't show themselves to me, I'll just use my imagination. Maybe if I get really close, they'll show up, and we can become friends."

Barrie was bored, and he suddenly found Felicity's idea intriguing. "That sounds like it would be fun. Would you like some help?"

Felicity held up her hand towards the saucers. "I told you I'd find out what you looked like. Now my brother is going to help me, and he knows everything."

Barrie grinned as he sat on the edge of the lounger. "So, where do we start?"

Felicity turned and looked at her brother. She hadn't expected it, but he seemed interested. She grinned and then bent her head as if deep in thought.

She lifted her markers and spread her paper out. "Let's begin with their body. We don't want to share their faces too early. It might scare them."

"OK, so how tall are they?"

"If they all have to live in that saucer for a long time, they must be pretty small.

Otherwise, they'd bump into each other."

"That makes sense, but have you thought about how they might have retractable legs so they can be both small and tall?"

Felicity squealed with delight. "OK, let's make them round like a ball but with legs that they can stick out when they want to be tall." She began to paint on her artist's tablet.

They continued to exchange ideas back and forth. Soon they had four round creatures, one with extended legs, and the other three used their extended arms to work the screens or pull themselves around the saucer.

"That's pretty good," Barrie said, "but they have to have some type of head."

"How about," said Felicity, "we put their head like a retractable box at the top of their body?"

"OK," said Barrie, sort of caught up in the project, "so their head is like an expandable box, depending on how smart they are, and it just pops up when they want to say or see something."

"Barrie, do you think they might get pretty lonely up there all that time?"

"They could be," said Barrie. "Maybe they read minds, and we can send nice thoughts to cheer them up."

Felicity flipped over on her back and reached toward the sky. "We," she said slowly, "want to be your friends. We could be nice to each other."

"If you visited us, we could have corn on the cob and hot fudge sundaes. Wouldn't you like that?"

Barrie put his hand out and patted his sister's arm. "That's really nice, Felicity. I hope they heard it."

Felicity suddenly shot up from the lounge. "What's that saying Mom always uses when she wants to encourage me to paint? I think it goes, 'A picture is worth a thousand words."

"Yeah, she is always saying that. What have you got in mind?"

"Bring the paint," Felicity said with excitement. We'll go

out to the bubble walls, and I'll paint my picture of them on the bubble. And just in case, we can also paint some nice words near the picture. So, they can have it both ways."

Barrie was about to reject the invitation, but when he saw his sister's excitement, he said, "Sure, why not?"

And so, the great artist and her faithful assistant journeyed to the bubble wall. Felicity was so excited she almost skipped along, and Barrie had to increase his pace to keep up.

When they reached the bubble wall, they spread a canvas, and Barrie unfolded a table. Felicity carefully laid out her colors and brushes. Then she began to paint. Only this time, her strokes were long, and with increasing confidence, she recreated her images of the visitors along with words of welcome.

Barrie had to admit that his sister's artistic skills were expanding. Soon they had a large scene that included both the earth and the saucers, and there were lots of hearts and smiles that floated between the earth and the saucers.

"See, Woo Woo," Felicity shouted towards the saucers hovering above the city. "You and Wonderrama better learn to speak English so we can invite you to be our neighbors. If you do that, we could have lots of fun and learn how to support each other. My Aunt's a pretty good nurse. You might need a nurse sometime, and it would be better if she already knew you."

"Who is WooWoo and Wonderama?"

"Oh, I just made that up," said Felicity. "I figured we all have to have names if we are going to get to know each other. If those names are wrong, they can always correct me and tell me their real names." She grinned and began to giggle. "You don't think they'll be upset, do you?"

"No," said Barrie, "I think they'll like it and like you for giving them names. It sure makes them less scary than being called aliens or even visitors."

While he had always been fond of his sister, he realized as they walked back towards their home that he both liked her and admired her spunk. In this day and age, he thought, it's nice to have a friend like that. And, he thought, it's especially nice if she is your sister.

With lots of laughter, giggles, and poking, they finally made it home. It would soon be time for supper, and both agreed that they had some homework and other things to catch up on. Their parents observed their entry with a quizzical look on their faces, but each had a big smile that they seemed to be enjoying each other so much.

CHAPTER 17
LIVING IN A BUBBLE

"In one way, people are always living in their own bubbles, but in another sense, even good life in a bubble still feels caged in," said Brooke.

"Life seems to be on hold. We're just waiting to see what our visitors will decide and do," Kara added.

They had chosen to pull away for a sanity break. Brooke, a hospital counselor, had mentioned that she was seeing signs of rising stress among her clients. "People need to have objectives and dreams as part of our DNA. Just standing around waiting is not healthy.

My husband, Derek, did a series of sermons about people traveling across the wilderness. The wilderness was rough and dangerous, but being connected with God gave them a goal and purpose in life. That makes sense to me. I counsel people in the hospital who have lost their sense of purpose in life. Believe me, we are healthiest when reaching for a promised land."

"What would be the best Promised Land to reach for given our present situation?" said Kara. They agreed to think about it and to meet for coffee in a week. When they regrouped, Kara said, “I guess a major feature of my Promised Land would be to find ways to clearly demonstrate our value as human beings.”

“So far, the Council has been working on getting the institutions in our city to behave in a way that demonstrates the value of residents,” said Kara. “Maybe we could encourage residents to practice that discipline of learning about the characteristics of the different cultures in our city and, in the process, demonstrate our openness to our visitors.”

“If we got residents to reach across our human separations and learn about each other, it would help prepare for our encounter with the visitors. The mayor could challenge all residents to cross one or two barriers with other residents as a way of preparing now for that time when we would have to reach across the great division and communicate with the aliens from another part of the universe?”

“So, we would encourage residents to heal some of the current divisions within our city as preparation for that day sometime in the future when we would use those skills to talk to the visitors,” said Kara. “That would be a win-win situation. If, of course, we could get our residents to act on that possibility.”

They were both excited and anxious to share with Derek to get his response. Kara suggested they could meet for dinner, and she would invite a rather progressive friend she had met at the college where she was teaching. They agreed to meet at a steak house that had managed to stay open and mysteriously found steaks in their freezer. It had become a popular gathering place for many associated with Kara's college.

The presence of fresh food at various restaurants and groceries was an unexplainable mystery of what was now a little over a two-year experience within their bubble. "Has anyone tried to stay in one of those freezers overnight and see how the supply doesn't seem to dwindle?" asked Brooke.

"Actually," said Kara, "there have been several attempts to answer that question, but none with any success."

"However, it happens. It does suggest that our visitors have some sense of what humans like and need and have made it available to us," said Brooke. "Like Moses got water from the rock, we get meat and vegetables from our freezer. Both are miracles. If we get this conversation thing worked out, that is one question I want answered."

"This whole experience has raised some faith questions as well for me. If God is the God of the universe, as my husband would say, then God is also the God of our visitors, whether they recognize it or not."

"That's deep, Brooke. Tell me more."

"I'm not a Biblical scholar, like my husband, but it stands to reason that those first Israelites who crossed that wilderness heading for the promised land made connections with people along the way and shared their belief in God with them. What if we are to do the same with our visitors?"

"Yikes, that is a scary thought. Do your children have some ideas about how to do that?"

"Not that they have told me. But think about it. If we did establish a friendly relationship with them, what would we want to have as part of that relationship?"

"I'd want to know more about them. What is their origin? Do they have faith, and if so, what is it? How do they see the future? And I'd also want them to know the same about us."

"That's a good beginning," said Brooke. "Huh, you know, when I think about it, having that type of exchange with other cultures in our world would make a better climate."

"Maybe we could practice that discipline with the different cultures in our city and, in the process, demonstrate it to our visitors. They seem to observe what we do down here even if they don't respond."

"Earlier, we were talking about the effect of people not having any objectives or ways to prepare for our encounter with the visitors. What if we offered the city the challenge of preparing now for that time when we would have to reach across the great division and communicate with the aliens from another part of the universe?"

"So, we would encourage residents to heal some of the current divisions within our city as preparation for that day sometime in the future when we would use those skills to talk to the visitors," said Kara. "That would be a win-win situation. If, of course, we could get our residents to act on that possibility."

"OK, to test that out, what would you like to know more about with our African American neighbors or our Hispanic or Asian neighbors?"

Brooke pulled out a notebook and a pen. "Let's make a list, but if we can convince the council, let's broadcast the idea and encourage others to do it. We could even have a contest for those who mutually produced the most surprising information."

They were both excited and anxious to share with Derek to get his response. Kara suggested they could meet for dinner, and she would invite a rather progressive friend she had casually dated from the college where she was teaching. They agreed to meet at a local steak house that had become a popular gathering place for many associated with Kara's college.

The Steak House raised another issue. "It never runs out of steaks. The presence of fresh food at various restaurants and groceries is among the unexplainable mysteries in our bubble. "Has anyone tried to stay in one of those freezers overnight and see how the supply doesn't seem to dwindle?" asked Brooke.

"Actually," said Kara, "there have been several attempts to answer that question, but none with any success."

"However it happens, it does suggest that our visitors have

some sense of what humans like and need and have made it available to us," said Brooke. "Like Moses got water from the rock, we get meat and vegetables from our freezer. Both are miracles. If we get this conversation thing worked out, I suspect that will be a major topic of conversation."

"Maybe our men folk will have some ideas. Anyway, let's set it up for this Friday evening," said Kara.

"Sounds like a plan," said Brooke. "Should I say anything about the content before we meet, or should we just see how they respond spontaneously?"

"Since Arthur will be hearing it for the first time at dinner, let's do the same with Derek,"

Both Brooke and Kara enjoyed teasing their companions that they had a big idea that would save the city but wanted to wait until they were together to reveal their idea.

When the introductions had been made, and they were seated and ordered their drinks and meals, Derek said. "OK, ladies, the preliminaries are over, and we are ready to hear this great idea."

Brooke nodded at Kara and asked, "Do you want me to introduce the idea? Then you can fill in any details I miss?"

With a sweep of the hand and a smile, Kara indicated her agreement, and Kara nodded.

"I'll get to our visitors in the sky, but first, let me ask both of you gentlemen to look around this restaurant and tell me any particular thing you notice."

Derek and Arthur glanced around the room, and Derek responded, "I see mostly couples or sometimes four people enjoying a good steak dinner, drinks, and each other's company. What are we supposed to see?"

"I would suggest that with one or two exceptions, most people are enjoying the company of people who are from the same race or culture as they are," said Kara.

Both men looked back around the room and then nodded their agreement. "Now that you mention it," said Arthur, "that seems to fit the pattern of our society. I've done a fair amount of work focused on the issue of racism and the tensions it creates in our society. Our research indicates that most of our population does not have significant social relationships with people of a different culture. We tend to hang with people who make us comfortable. Actually, it is not just with race, but economics, education, and other social divisions as well."

"I think I sense where this conversation might be headed," said Derek. "If we can't build relationships with people across small differences like race, economics, etc., how do we expect to relate to creatures from other parts of our universe?"

"Bingo," said Kara. "I always knew that you married a smart man, Brooke."

"Thanks, but that is only part of the idea we want to explore. "We've been doing a lot of experimenting in our city with ways our institutions affirm a person's worth. As far as I know, we have not taken any specific action to transcend our city's cultural and racial barriers. Yet race and culture have been the major divisions that separate us. The dominant party expects the minority parties to adapt to the norm that the powerful have established.

While we don't yet have any comfortable two-way communication with our visitors, what if we began by developing some skills in transcending our human barriers in preparation for when we could also apply them in communication with our visitors?"

"What an intriguing idea," said Arthur. "While I've done some work in that area, mostly we've worked with small groups of already committed individuals. This crisis has enabled our local government to ask institutions to step beyond their comfort levels and standardized thinking. What I hear the two of you suggesting is that we might also take advantage of our situation to explore something similar with our residents."

"You don't make bad choices in men yourself, Kara," said Brooke. "Yes, Arthur, that is exactly what we've been thinking about."

"I think we men have been complimented, so thank you, but the subject matter is even more fascinating. Our city in a bubble allows us to explore some possibilities that would eventually benefit our whole civilization and maybe even beyond. Please say more."

"Kara and I were having a little stress-reducing dinner together a couple of days ago, and we talked about what we would most want in our new future. It got me thinking about something Derek recently said in one of his sermons. He spoke about the importance of having a vision, to use the Biblical image, a Promised Land, which gives us courage as we travel through our own wilderness."

Kara spoke up. "When Brooke asked what some of the features of my Promised Land would be, I first said the obvious—that our visitors would leave us alone."

"But then I shared some of what our children are experiencing," said Brooke.

Arthur looked curious. "Your children?

"You may not have heard yet," said Derek, "but for reasons we can't fully understand, our children, particularly our daughter, Felicity, have been able to actually get a brief exchange from the ships."

"She what!" Arthur looked astonished.

"You'll hear the details at the Council meeting," said Brooke, "when we share our idea about building community with our visitors, but in brief, our children have received a response from the picture they drew on the bubble. It makes what we are talking about all the more important."

CHAPTER 18
THE NOURISHING FRUIT OF LISTENING

Two days later, Derek, Brooke, Kara, and Arthur met; this time in a conference room where they could spread out but also have privacy.

"I spoke to Eleanor about our idea of helping the city learn how to communicate with people who were different from them in preparation for the time when we can have a two-way exchange with our visitors. Of course, as an African American in a white-dominated society, that has been a major challenge for her throughout her life. She asked that we bring some rough ideas to the next Council meeting, scheduled for this Friday afternoon."

"What if we explained to the city that we need to practice building positive relationships with people who are distinctly different from us in preparation for the time when we will do the same with our saucer visitors?

"I've been thinking that a good way to begin among our earth neighbors," said Arthur, "would be for each party to affirm what they appreciate about the other person's culture, history, and giftedness. To hear those types of affirmation may lessen the anxiety that each of them feels."

"In the church," said Derek, "we speak of loving our neighbors as ourselves. When I speak of love, I am not talking about fuzzy feelings but rather focusing our energy on what we believe is best for that other person. So, another way to build the relationship is to offer something that is clearly focused on that other person's wellbeing."

"Both ideas are good ways to begin when our conversation partner lives in our community, but it gets more difficult when, like with our saucer friends, we don't know anything about their background. We will have to encourage our residents to take risks in reaching out to them."

"As we explain the idea to the city," said Kara, "I'd keep emphasizing this dual purpose—building better relationships within the city and making a positive connection with our space visitors," said Kara. "That way, as we experience some benefit from the first level, we begin to build confidence in the possibilities at the second level."

"How do you think earthlings can benefit from building connections with our space friends?" asked Brooke.

"There certainly can be ways that their advanced technology could help us manage some problems on Earth," said Arthur. "I also think every time we expand our knowledge about another person, at the same time, we learn more about ourselves. Relating to extra-terrestrials will teach us much about ourselves."

"Do you suppose by learning to overcome our fears relating to them, we might also strengthen our capacity to have peace on earth and even less crime?" said Kara.

"If we can build a hopeful vision of that happening, then we might have Victor Frankl's "WHY" that will give us the courage to help our visitors at the same time," said Derek.

"However, we have an additional hurdle to cross with the Visitors. How do you communicate with someone you are afraid of?" asked Kara.

"To return to the Biblical example that began this conversation, you start by offering gifts that show the other person to be a person of value. In the Abraham example, he killed the fatted calf, which offered something of value – a meal that both gives pleasure and nourishes the body," said Derek. "Of course, we first need to discover whether our visitors eat and what gives them pleasure."

"I'm reluctant to say it, but I think," said Brooke, "that our children may have provided us with a possible clue. When the visitors sent a response to our daughter, part of it was an offer of food, something that looked like a kind of apple. The very fact that they offered a kind of food as a gift would suggest that food is part of the nature of their lives."

Derek spoke up, "I have an idea of how to build on this theory. We suggest that the mayor invite people to reach out to five to ten people who are different from them. At the same time, why don't we encourage the children of our city to develop a variety of ways to offer food and other symbols of welcome to our visitors? As they respond, we will pick up some ideas of what they might like or dislike."

"Let's carry these ideas to the Council and see how they respond," said Kara.

"You know," said Brooke, "the more we talk about these ideas, the more excited I get and the more positive I feel about our visitors. If we can make the same thing happen for our city residents, and if it is true that our visitors can read our thoughts and feelings, we may have stumbled on to our best approach to creating a positive link between us."

"I think you are right," said Arthur, "but we also need to begin to think about and plan for how we respond if our visitors don't behave in a positive our efforts."

"Way to spoil a good mood," said Brooke. "Have you got any ideas about that?"

"I think it will help if we can provide everyone with simple guidelines," said Derek. Nothing very developed, but we have worked on that in my work around healing divisions in our society. One thing we've developed is adapting the procedure of the Truth and Reconciliation Commission from South Africa."

"Say more about that," said Kara.

"When Blacks were assuming power in South Africa,

Whites were afraid that Blacks would seek revenge for the ways that the White population had treated them," said Arthur.

"That would be an understandable fear," said Kara. "From what little I've read about South Africa, the Whites were very cruel and treated the Blacks almost like animals to keep them under their control. With the tables turned, I can see why they were afraid."

"The Truth and Reconciliation Commission was designed to prevent violent retaliation. They set up a series of hearings where two things happened at once. First, Blacks were invited to come before the commission and tell their story of what it had been personally like to live under the unjust rule of Apartheid. Putting words on their experience and knowing that people were actually listening to them seemed to provide them some healing and relief. After all, revenge is usually about having someone recognize the painful events in one's life.

"The second part of the commission was having those Whites that had exercised such cruelty sit before the commission and confess what they had done. To confess is to accept responsibility. Then, having confessed, they also asked for forgiveness so that they might live in society without fear. They wanted to move from being the author of cruel behavior towards others to once again becoming a productive citizen. While it was clearly driven by fear, they were able in the process to cleanse their souls at the same time."

"That sounds like a noble effort," said Brooke. "Did it work?"

"It was rather miraculous," said Derek. "South Africa moved from being like a time bomb waiting to explode to discovering productive possibilities as a society."

"So how do you propose to adapt that for our city?"

"What if the city held its own public hearings and streamed them across the entire city? We'd ask Black and other minorities in our city to simply tell the story of how they experienced discrimination and injustice while living there. Whether it was all real or, at times, a projection of their fears, they get to tell their story, and, most importantly, they get to be heard by their fellow citizens. Then, we'd ask White citizens to speak of what they have learned in listening to their neighbors tell their stories and, more importantly, what they wanted to do about it. For some, it will be the first experience to accept responsibility for what is happening in Wall Nut Cove and publicly vowing to do something about it."

"One thing we have explored in my work," said Arthur, "is the power of story to interrupt a chain of thinking and open new possibilities. We are proposing that people be given the possibility to have others hear their stories about the pain of their lives.

"You might have some ideas about that, Derek. Wasn't that

part of Jesus' strategy when he crafted his parables?"

"We might even draw upon the gifts of our residents and have a parable writing contest and see who can develop the best parables that address the pain and injustice of racism, both personal and systemic," said Brooke.

"Wow," said Eleanor, "my head is spinning with all these ideas. I think it may be time for us to take a break and try to pull together our notes in preparation for the Council meeting."

"Arthur, can you sketch a brief framework for such honest conversations?"

"Sure, I'd be glad to."

"Kara, would you be willing to have some conversations about the food-sharing idea?"

"Sure. I think it could be fun."

"Of course, the key will be getting a response from our visitors that we can build upon. But hopefully, this may offer a positive response to our citizens."

"Heh! It just occurred to me," said Eleanor, "that we have been overlooking an important fact. We've been at this for over two years, and our visitors have chosen to communicate with us only three times."

"I know," said Jess, "it is very frustrating. What are they waiting for?"

"That's a good question, Jess, but that is not why I brought it up. My point is, in all that time, with whom have they chosen to communicate?"

"What do you mean, Eleanor?"

"They have only chosen to communicate with a preacher and children. Why is that?"

"Well, the preacher I get, he's in the communication business," said Jess."

"Don't dismiss the children," said Eleanor. "We do that all the time in our society. What if something unique about children made them especially open to our visitors? I mean, think about it, what are some of the main communication features children use?"

"If my daughter is an example," said Brooke, "she knows no boundaries, is hopelessly optimistic, communicates in short sentences, laughter, stories, and thinks the best of everyone."

"Actually, when you think about it, preachers use some of those same features," said Jess.

"My children have caused me to think in a different direction."

That Scripture passage about letting a little child lead us if we want to enter the Kingdom has certainly been proved in this case. What are they saying?"

"Felicity, who is our eternal optimist, has, as you've heard, established a form of two-way communication. She has even given a couple of them names—she calls them Woo Woo and Wonderama. I'll never know where she came up with those, but in the last exchange, they actually responded by using those names."

"What's the point of all of this?" said Jess.

"The point is," said Eleanor, "that in the second part of my broadcast, why don't I invite the children of our city to use their gifts to provide a welcome for our visitors?"

"The mayor can issue an invitation in the second part of her broadcast, and we can see what they come up with," said Brooke.

CHAPTER 19
A CHILDLIKE RESPONSE

Barrie was shooting hoops with friends at a nearby park when he heard the loud squeal of his sister as she ran up to him, calling his name.

"Barrie, they answered. Come see, WooWoo and Wonderrama answered."

Barrie dropped the ball and ran to where she was. "Slow down and catch your breath. What do you mean they answered?"

"They sent their own picture. Come and see, "she squealed as she grabbed his hand and ran back towards the bubble wall where they had left her painting.

Barrie stopped and stared. He could hardly believe his eyes. There was a second painting next to Felicity's painting, but this time on the outside of the bubble. It displayed a replica of a couple of flying saucers with planets and stars in the background.

Attached to a flying saucer was a rough image of a little girl on a bike with her hand reaching out to a round ball with a square face that was reaching toward her.

The alien held what looked like a large juicy apple in his hand, and next to it were the words WooWoo and Wonderama.

There was also a large heart next to some floating bubbles in three different colors. The color of the bubbles was slightly different from the colors that Barrie recognized. They were a strange form of green/and red and another one brown and purple.

“You did it!” Barrie screamed at Felicity. “Come on. We’ve got to go and tell Dad.

At first, when they came screaming into the house, they were so excited that Derek had trouble understanding them. Then their words penetrated his brain, and he ran out the door towards the bubble with them trailing behind.

When he arrived at the bubble wall, he stood in shock and had trouble processing what was on the bubble. He turned towards the sky where the saucers hovered and shouted towards them. “Why! Why have you chosen my family to be your funnel for conversation? We are not that special, you know.”

Then the practical side of his personality began to function. He immediately pulled out his phone and dialed the mayor.

When she answered, his first words were, “Eleanor, are you alone, and are you sitting down?”

“Ever since I met you, I’ve learned I must be prepared for almost anything. What is it now, Derek?”

“We’ve received another communication from our neighbors. They’ve chosen to use their picture to communicate with my children.”

"Your children!"

"I can't believe it either, but let me try to explain what has happened. My precocious daughter decided that since we weren't communicating by words, maybe she could help out by painting a picture of welcome on the bubble wall. And darn it, Eleanor, it worked. If you go out to the bubble on the east side of the city near the small pond on 22nd street, you will find both Felicity's painting and what looks like a clear response from the saucer people."

"Yikes! I'm on my way. Meet me there. I'll also have my secretary call some of the council. This could be a big breakthrough."

When the mayor arrived, Derek tried to describe what may have led to this.

"Her mother always encouraged her to practice her art skills by repeatedly saying, 'A picture is worth a thousand words.' So, one day she decided to test that saying by taking her paints out to the bubble wall and painting a picture for our visitors. I don't quite understand the next part, but she also gave them names—WooWoo and Wonderama.

"While we still have no idea about what they actually look like, they chose to use one of her images of them to communicate."

"That is another proof that they are aware of what we are saying down here, or at least what some of us are saying, and they are responsive," said Jess. "That is really crucial."

"Makes sense to me," said Eleanor, "but we just discovered this and haven't figured out how to use it to communicate."

At least we now know that it is possible," said Derek.

"Just remember, whatever is in those ships, they are totally different from anyone or anything that we have ever experienced. We live on a planet that can't even get beyond skin color and slightly different cultures. How do we learn to transcend our fears and vast differences?" asked Antonio.

"Once again," said Kara, "we've been given some time to develop our skills in communicating across differences before we have to exercise those skills to communicate with them. It's like they are helping to prepare us ahead of time. Am I dreaming, or are there some signs of compassion here?"

"Again, we have the advantage of having a confined group of residents who are so aware of our mutual threat that they might be willing to explore what it might mean to combine our diverse gifts in preparation for reaching far beyond ourselves."

"So how do we learn to communicate in a way that enables us to step beyond our fears and open ourselves to the rich diversity of our universe?" asked Antonio.

"Derek," said Brooke, "You're always preaching about the ethic of hospitality as a key element of our faith. Expand on that Biblical story that you often refer to that emphasizes the gift of hospitality."

"Well, I'll be. My wife even listens to me when I preach."

"We'll debate about who listens to whom at another time. For now, what is the Biblical story about hospitality?"

"It's in Genesis where Abraham is sitting near the Oak of Mamre when three strangers suddenly confront him." The natural response would be to run away or attack them first. Instead of acting out of fear to protect himself and his family, he extends abundant hospitality. He has his prized fatted calf killed and prepared for a banquet for his guests. He's demonstrating the value in which the guests are held.

Then, several verses later, we are told that Abraham exhibits another one of faith's virtues that we find difficult to practice. He began to beg and negotiate with God on behalf of the residents of Sodom and Gomorrah."

"So, we are saying that hospitality and compassion for the stranger is an essential part of our faith," said Brooke. "Can it also be part of our city's values?"

"Exactly," said Antonio, "How do we help our residents reach across their differences and build a community that enriches all of us? They didn't do so well with that challenge with my people in the past."

"Now we have a different reality with the saucers. We suggest," said Arthur, "that we practice with humans relating to humans of different cultures. Then when that day arrives, we can apply those experiences to shape our response to the visitors?"

"I just thought of something," said Derek, with growing excitement. "I'm not sure how far to expand on the Biblical story, but in Hebrews, Abraham was actually welcoming some non-earthly beings in that experience.

"Hebrews speaks of Abraham meeting 'angels unaware.' It's sort of ironic that we might be having a parallel experience. Not judging whether our visitors fit into the angel category or something entirely different, but aren't the parallels rather tantalizing?

"Let's play with this metaphor," said Brooke. "What might it mean to express hospitality and compassion to our visitors, especially when we don't know their intentions toward us?"

"I think hospitality is expressed best," said Derek, "when you act towards another in a way that clearly demonstrates that you have their best interests at heart. The problem is, we don't understand what our visitors like, fear, or even tolerate."

"That's not quite true," said Brooke. "We've had several examples that suggest they have the capacity for compassion and even fairness."

"And," said Kara, "they seem to have the capacity to be both patient and tolerant. I mean, with their technology, they could have blown us off the planet after that missile fiasco, and yet, they only sent a cryptic message and continued to patiently see how we would develop over the next few years."

“While we are focused on trying to help adults gain new skills in reaching across differences, maybe we might have children try out different ways to express kindness and care for our visitors. They seem to have a natural gift for doing that together.”

“Go back to Felicity’s experience,” said Kara. “The first response to Felicity’s picture included a gift of some type of food, sort of like an apple. Maybe different groups of children can prepare various food dishes that are spread out in that same field where the saucerites previously burned their message.”

“Oh, I like that. Instead of fear, it shows a welcoming atmosphere.”

“And if we kept a watch on how they responded to each offering, we might think of other possible ways to respond with kindness and care.”

CHAPTER 20
THE MAYOR CHALLENGES THE RESIDENTS

Derek saw the weariness on the faces of the Council as the four of them entered the conference room for the mayor's announcement. It was one thing to convince the various institutions of the city to refocus their energy on how to help the individuals that came to them, but now they were going to explore an even more difficult task of individuals being continually aware of the well-being of others.

Antonio, a fourth-generation immigrant from Mexico, spoke up. "How do you convince the city's residents to voluntarily make themselves more vulnerable by reaching out to people who have historically been separated from one another? That has always been a challenge in this city and others."

"African Americans have faced that for over four-hundred years," said Eleanor. "And we are far more alike than we are with the visitors.

Once they were seated, the mayor continued. "We are now two and a half years into this experience—about halfway through our projected five-year challenge. I think that we have made some significant progress with the institutions of our city having shifted their mindset from 'what's in it for us' to ‘what’s in it for those who come to us.’”

“Am I correct in assuming we are about to consider a different type of challenge today?” said Jess.

“Yes, Derek and Kara, plus their two guests, have been examining the next phase of our journey,” said the mayor. “You may be aware that there are indications that we are approaching a new phase when we will be hearing from our visitors more directly.”

“Hallelujah, it’s about time,” said Eric.

“Maybe hallelujah,” said Eleanor, “but consider what that means. What if our guests did decide to visit us, and when they do, they look like monsters and literally breathe fire when they talk?”

“We’ve already got several vigilante groups who are storing their weapons when that day arrives,” said Eric.

“Since the ships have not directly attacked us, even acted with compassion a couple of times,” said Kara, “why do you think we have citizens that are preparing for war?”

“It’s pretty obvious, isn’t it,” said Jess. “They may not have attacked us, but they have done little to build our trust. When you are afraid of others, the first response is to protect yourself. That’s just human nature.”

“And if we respond with defensiveness and maybe even aggression, given their advanced technology, what do you think the results will be?” asked Brooke.

“Not pretty,” said Eric, “but you must do something to protect yourself. If they want to be friendly, they got to do more than save a few cats caught in traffic.”

“Derek came to me a couple of weeks ago suggesting we may want to begin now to explore a different approach,” said Eleanor. “I’ll let him explain it.”

“Let me begin by thanking each of you for all the effort and ingenuity that you have offered the city these last two and one-half years. Because of your efforts, we are a better city, but as we approach the five-year mark, we must face another major issue.”

“You know my wife, Brooke, and of course, Kara, but I’d like to introduce you to Arthur McPherson. Arthur is a researcher and professor at our nearby university. The last couple of years, he has worked with various people on how to transcend and heal the divisions in our society.”

“As you know,” said Kara, “I came to this country from India. Let me tell you, the transition was not easy. Not only did I have the normal barriers of language and societal habits, but I also had the additional barriers of assumptions about foreigners and cultural biases. Male attitudes towards women and the current debates over immigration are both a continual part of my life.”

“As we approach our five-year mark, we will be confronted by our ability to communicate across the largest barrier ever—

residents from different planets. The history of humanity is one of division and separation—frequently on the basis of either race or culture. Our hope is to engage in practices that might heal the divisions that exist in our city.

Examples of those divisions are racial, ethnic, economic, and religious, and you could add others to the list. Think about it. Those divisions are all among our central identity as humans. The challenge we will eventually face is building a community with non-human beings. We do that so that we may strengthen our relationship by building muscles.

We want to use our experience to prepare all of us to communicate with our visitors in a way that doesn't cause division but builds bonds of community and trust."

"The difference," said Derek, "is that this time we aren't working with a dozen institutions but every resident in our city."

"So," said Jess, "you're suggesting that we practice reaching across our human divisions as preparation for reaching across our planetary divisions. Rather ambitious, I'd say, but I'm not sure we have much choice."

"Our idea is that first, we explain why we are doing this, but then we ask each resident to participate in activities that heal our divisions, and then we broadcast what we have learned and apply it to our interplanetary situation. We need each resident to help us build the best community bonds possible.

In essence, each of them is a key element in a future rarely imagined outside of religious visions.

"As you know, our mayor has worked with the broadcast media in our town to establish a special channel by which the whole city can communicate with each other. We also suggest that you report the results of your experience, including the problems you are having, on this special channel to build momentum and confidence," said Kara.

"This is where our task becomes a little more difficult. We have just tried to explain why we are asking you to take this on. We build into the process a report and feedback mechanism so that any given time we know, and hopefully our visitors know, what we are attempting," said Arthur.

"We also want to build in a game-like experience so that it also becomes fun to participate," said Derek. "Let's begin at the beginning. We propose a celebratory newscast to celebrate all we have accomplished so far. We should feel good as a city about what we have been able to accomplish in the last couple of years. Our prison is a reformatory, and hardened criminals are discovering a new lease on life. Courts have converted punishment into paths of transformation."

"We have developed a whole new economic system with our businesses humming again. And our schools are full of vital students and teachers who demonstrate how to think for themselves daily. I don't know what our visitors will decide to do with us, but our young people will adapt and carve out a future that cares about the planet and each other. I'll bet if some of their planets knew how to think that freely, they wouldn't need to seek new planets to populate," said Antonio.

"And exactly how are you going to be able to do that?" asked Eric.

"Let me ask you a question. My research " said Arthur, "suggests that very few people have close friends from other cultures or races. Consider yourselves. Before this all began, how many of you had deep friendships with people from another race or culture?"

Kara and Eleanor raised their hands but admitted that they still reached out to people from their same culture for their most intimate sharing.

"Even before this all began, you were a fairly open-minded city. And yet, when we reflect on it, many of us did not have close friends from other ethnic groups. How do we expect to build a diverse community when we don't let people who differ from us into our hearts and souls?

"We want to take advantage of the pressures of our short future to see if we can discover the strength of our diversity. We are reminded that we only have a year or so to prepare ourselves to build friendships with non-earthlings so that each of us can benefit from the other. I'll let Arthur explain the first steps."

"At the end of our confidence-building celebration, we'll ask all residents to enter a training program that builds up their relation-building muscles. Each person does that by identifying at least ten people of different backgrounds and cultures. When they leave the stadium, they will approach those people and ask them if they are willing to explore a possible in-depth friendship.

Everyone will have heard the same broadcast in the city, so they will know that all this is in preparation for eventually exploring friendships with our visitors. They will begin by discussing similar subjects.

When a resident has had six to ten such conversations, they will be asked to summarize what they have learned about healing division in our city and express what they are willing to do to reach out to our visitors.

We will summarize the city's conclusions about the next steps for everyone to read.

"I must admit that I didn't believe you could ever get the majority of city residents to follow that in normal times. However, as we have discussed in the last couple of years, the threat of those ships overhead, and their absolute refusal to communicate either positively or negatively, makes such an approach a possibility," said Eleanor.

"Once again, the threat of the end of our world opens up some new and beneficial possibilities," said Derek. "We'll have to pull together quite a crew to summarize the responses, but if they are all sent in by computer, the project is possible, and I think the residents will benefit from seeing the results."

"Copies of these questions will be made available for all our residents. We can also offer at least 100 prizes for those who develop the most viable strategy for building relationships both in our city and with our visitors," said Antonio.

"We were thinking that we might put forth the challenge on our weekly broadcast and see what our population comes up with," said Brooke.

Derek turned towards Eleanor. "Shall I spring the next surprise on them, madam mayor?"

Eleanor smiled and said, "We are going to pause for a commercial break. It will allow each of you to stretch, take a bathroom break, and call a personal friend. Then, after fifteen minutes, we will reconvene. We'll continue with what Derek is referencing. While it is very serious, I think you will have some fun examining it. We could use some fun, so I look forward to having you return."

Arthur, who had been observing the council's response, turned to Kara and said. "I think you will find that with each positive step that people take, the more energy they will have and the more relaxed they will become. The kidding back and forth also adds an important dimension to what is happening."

"Thanks, Arthur. You have been a great help. I've been

considering inviting you to an event for other reasons, but I'm glad this opportunity arose for us to work together." She smiled and excused herself to get a Danish in preparation for the next phase.

CHAPTER 21
SHARING FOOD AND JOY

The Mayor began her news conference on a somber note.

"It's a strange thing about feelings and moods. You can walk along performing your daily tasks, and someone will say something, or something will happen and suddenly, your mood changes dramatically. The people of Walnut Cove had been in a perpetual state of terror for over two years now. Many showed signs of what was called 'post-traumatic stress.' People rarely smiled anymore, and their tempers flared at the slightest provocation. They tuned in to our daily broadcast each day, but they rarely expected to hear any significant good news.

Our effort to transform the Institutions of our city into people-serving agencies has had beneficial results. People, not institutions, have felt valued. Still, every time we dared to have a positive thought, we simply looked up and saw the ships hovering in the sky above. The immediate threat has disappeared, but we know that in an instant, it can return, and there is nothing we can do about it.

Eleanor paused, then focused directly on the camera and continued. "Welcome back, my friends.

"Let me reveal to you an incident that occurred recently that encourages me to believe that we may be approaching a time to have two-way communication with our visitors. I'll describe the incident in just a moment, but first, let me provide some context.

"First, consider appearances. What happens when you see a group of people who look, talk, and act in ways that are totally different from you? Take a piece of paper or a dictating machine and make a list of five to ten thoughts or behaviors that people from one group often have concerning people who are different from them."

Kara leaned over towards Derek and said in a low voice, "Gee, that's the type of exercise you would give out. You don't suppose you are infectious, do you?

The Mayor continued. "Review that list and note how if one group has more power and/or wealth than the other, they frequently exercise that power to protect what they have rather than build relationships. Our country does not have a positive experience in reaching across our differences. I've been honored to be your first African Mayor, but if you look around the country, I'm the exception rather than the norm.

At this point, I remind you of this because at a point in time when we are about to encounter a life form that is totally different from any of us, we have not been very skilled in reaching across barriers of difference. Consider our history with Native Americans, Africans, Asians, and Hispanic immigrants.

Our visitors have communicated with us that they are not as focused on our past as our future behavior. You don't begin new behavior perfectly. We learn new skills through trial and error and lots of practice and forgiveness.

We invite every resident to strengthen their relationship muscles with other residents before we apply it to our visitors. So, your assignment, should you choose to accept it, is to practice reaching across the division between yourself and one or more of those divisions.

If we are to have a positive experience in meeting our visitors, we will have to learn how to avoid those thoughts and behaviors that separate and build on that which unites." Therefore, we invite every resident of Walnut Cove to engage in the following exercise.

"Start small and identify five to ten people different from you and try to build a relationship with them. I think you will discover there is value in owning some of the negative possibilities and ask your new friends to help you avoid those actions and behaviors that have historically strained your relationships. If you genuinely listen to each other's response, you will find yourselves growing closer.

"I know from both positive and some very negative experiences," said Eleanor, that the wounds are painful, but the healing can produce abundant fruits. Compile your list of positive behaviors and send them to the mayor's office. We will share them with the city in preparation for when we do meet our new friends. We have an opportunity to positively affect our community and, in the process, prepare ourselves for our future."

Here is a suggested list of topics. We will keep a recording of them on this station, or if you send us your email, we'll send you a printed copy. Imagine what it might mean if every city resident spoke about this to others but truly listened to others respond as well.

BUILDING TRUST AND FRIENDSHIP

* What types of fears and insecurities might prevent us from being vulnerable to each other?

* What steps can we take to overcome that fear?

* How might we benefit from our relationship if we could overcome our fears and get to know each other in-depth?

* How might this be true in our relationship with our visitors?

* What might make you hesitant about my knowing your deepest secrets?

* What could I do to overcome your concerns?

* How might I help our visitors overcome their concerns about letting us know their inner secrets?

* What would be the benefits of our two cultures totally

trusting that the other group only wanted the best for us?

* How might we begin to help our visitors see those same benefits?

* What could you and I do to express to our visitors that we want a deeper relationship and want to give up our fears and welcome them?

Eleanor continued to explain. "About a year ago, we became aware of some demands made by our visitors. Derek Mansfield, pastor of the Walnut Cove Presbyterian Church, came to me to report his strange encounter with our visitors, who informed him that the city had five years to demonstrate our worth as human beings. If we didn't measure up, we would be replaced by a population from another planet.

Your Council developed a plan that we have been implementing throughout the city. I am very proud of their work and think they have served you well. However, we continue to have no message communication with our visitors.

The purpose of this broadcast is to help each of us to prepare for that day in the future when we will have the opportunity to interact with our visitors. We have recently discovered that in addition to the communication with the Reverend Mansfield, there has also been an interaction with his two children, Brian and Felicity. Those two sets of communication provide us with some information about our visitors.

"First of all, though we don't know if they have a faith,

the interaction with the Reverend Mansfield suggests that at least they have some respect for religion, and a couple of other incidents would suggest that, regardless of whether they have a faith of their own, or not, they do have a sense of compassion and fairness.

"In addition, it is interesting that they chose to respond to children for their second attempt to communicate. It is on the basis of their seeming preference for children and their ethic of fairness that we are making the following suggestion as to our next steps.

Now, let us admit the unspoken thought that most of us carry around in our hearts and souls. We don't know how or when it will happen, but someday our visitors will show themselves. What will it be like when we earthlings and our visitors from a faraway universe first see each other? Will they be giant figures that swat at earthlings like we swat at flies? Or will they be shimmering pillars of light that flash rather than speak? If we perceive that any of their behavior is less than friendly, how can we respond in a way that transforms the negative into a positive?

"How will we communicate if we don't have the same language? Will our first response be to have all sorts of military equipment around, or will we prostrate ourselves and quake in fear? Or can we demonstrate a welcome that encourages them to explore the positive possibilities that might emerge from what we can contribute to each other?

"We do know that they seem to understand what we're saying and doing here in Walnut Cove. Therefore, the question is, what do we want to convey to them?

"Your mayor and council suggest we use this small window of time that we have and practice non-threatening greetings. In fact, since our visitors seem to prefer children, we thought it might be wise to invite the children of Walnut Cove to help us prepare our welcome.

"Our initial thoughts are that children should display several forms of greeting. Maybe some special foods, a musical presentation or two, and perhaps a big sign in bright colors that encourages them to come in peace and friendship. Some have suggested we use that big field on the edge of the city, and we have a variety of foods and gifts available.

"We might also have a variety of very cute pets and some dancers to show us how to dance and sing at the same time.

"Those are just some suggestions. We'll let the children of the city decide and report to us. If they want to, they can use our field to display any subject or activity they choose.

"I encourage you young people in our city to display hospitality, and I urge you adults to reach out to other cultures, races, and religions. Together we can provide a rich experience. If someone says they don't want to participate, ask them to tell you why, and listen, listen, listen. We are discovering that we are a richer city than we knew.

"As a beginning, might I encourage any interested young person to bring their ideas to Covington Field today at 12:30. I have arranged for a variety of pizzas and drinks to be available at no cost to you.

"We'll sign off for now. We'll see many of you at Covington Field, and we will also have cameras set up so that those who cannot come can see what is taking place. If you believe in prayer, I invite you to keep the city and all of its residents in your prayers. If you do not engage in prayer, just keep your city in your most positive thoughts."

CHAPTER 22
WELCOMING THE STRANGER

Seventeen-year-old Barrie and his twelve-year-old sister, Felicity, were immediately selected as the organizers. Earlier, Barrie had told his dad, "Dad, what are we going to do? I don't know anything about organizing hospitality events."

Derek, who had felt rather overwhelmed by being the center of attention, looked at Brian for several seconds before responding.

"Brian, I don't think anyone can explain why our family has been singled out as key people in what is happening. What I do know is that no one has all the answers, so we just do the best we can."

"But there will be lots of kids at Covington field, each with their own crazy ideas, some of which might even be very good. How do we take it all in?"

"First, we know the saucer people are listening, so let them gather the information. Second, why don't you suggest everyone divide themselves around special projects?

You can have a food group.

Next, have a WELCOME message and sign group.

Then why don't you have a music and dance group—that's

always good to help people feel welcome.

Include a pet group that allows people to show off their pets.

Maybe you could have a scary picture group to build on Felicity's idea that until you find out otherwise, you'll make up what they look like and how scary they can be.

Let them meet, eat pizza, and plan for a few hours. Then have a rally where everyone can report in. Keep reminding them that the major theme is how we make our visitors feel welcome and less scary."

"Thanks, Dad. Felicity, why don't you help coordinate the food, pictures, and welcome sign groups? I'll get some friends to help organize the pets, music, and how to convince them that we aren't scary, just different than they are.

People began arriving at about 11 a.m. They were in a good mood and headed straight for the food kiosks to get their pizzas. Barrie had signs erected that pointed to the spots where the different groups gathered.

Each group had a leader with basic instructions as to how the groups were to proceed. The rather miraculous thing is how well the different age groups listened and cooperated.

The scary picture group was the most creative. Felicity was in charge of them, and they quickly spread-out paper or canvases and began to paint or draw the scariest creatures they could imagine.

Everyone was familiar with Felicity's original painting. Some of them tried to copy that, but others moved off in new directions.

The news station filmed the activities and had a live feed to report on each group. Delilah, a fifteen-year-old, brought her music group with her. They offered to present a new song they had written for the occasion. The theme of the song was how feelings of terror turned into delight when you added a nice tune and feet-tapping rhythm.

The tune was simple, and the newscasters broadcast it and encouraged those at home to sing along. Soon the whole stadium was alive with joy and hope. And for those who watched from home, many opened their doors so their neighbors could join them.

The music group provided both the words and the music to be put on the screen and posted on the large stadium electronic board.

"Love Thy Neighbor"

1. "In our heart of hearts, we know it's true.
These saucerites come from afar.
To find a home that's really new.
To help neighbors from a different star.

****

2. The Saucers are filled with scary dudes
With pointy ears and teeth that shine.

Their musical tone changes attitudes.
And soon with food we sit to dine.
****

3. Some day we hope to fly.
Across the space that separates us.
To give our neighbors a great big hi.
And spread love that Jesus bids us try.
****

Soon, members of the Council and other adults joined in to the song and laughter. Some even tried to write new verses that could also be introduced on the fly.

Suddenly another group of instruments began to play as they marched down the field. Behind them came the sign group with a welcome banner in bright colors and large letters. Many hearts and flowers proclaimed a large welcome to their new neighbors. These were followed by a long procession of pets who seemed entranced by the events.

Derek turned to the Mayor. This is really great. Of course, we don't know how long it will be before or if our visitor will come, but it has felt good for the city to come together. On the one hand, it's like we were all enjoying ourselves at a city-wide party. And some of the ideas they have come up with to display welcome are unbelievable. Rather than fearing what will happen next, it's almost like we are looking forward to their coming.

Antonio approached the two of them. He wrapped his arms around both of them and let out a yelp. "Look at that down there. There are plenty of differences, but they also have discovered how to come together and enrich each other.

"Eleanor, imagine what your great-grandparents would have thought of this. I know mine would have wondered if the Kingdom had come."

Derek looked up into the sky. "I wonder what they are thinking now?"

"Madam Mayor, why don't we announce that we will gather again in three days? Tell them they are all invited to come with some form of welcome for our visitors. It can be verbal, physical, emotional—anything that says that if you don't come and visit us soon, you are really going to miss out on some wonderful things," said Anthony.

"That's really a good idea," said Derek. "Why don't you make your way to the microphone, and I'll alert the news broadcasters."

"Let me build on that. Let's let Anthony, Michal, and maybe we could invite some Asians, Kara from India, and several others to join us in the announcement," said Eleanor.

CHAPTER 23
AN ECHO OF HISTORY

History doesn't repeat itself, but sometimes you hear an echo from history that helps you find meaning and even purpose in the chaotic present. Once before, Derek recalled, a seemingly insignificant event occurred in an out-of-the-way village of a third-rate colony of the Roman empire. An out-of-wedlock woman gave birth to a child in a straw-filled shed because the parents were so unimportant that they couldn't even find space for them at the local inn. The wealthy and the powerful decision makers that shaped the world didn't even know that the event took place, and yet the world was changed.

Derek was afraid to voice it, but he wondered if he and the world were experiencing an echo of that event so long ago in Nazareth. He didn't think for a moment that God had arranged this Saucer event for some divine purpose, but he also didn't believe that events controlled God. If God is Lord of History, how might God be working through this event for some greater purpose?

Like in Nazareth so long ago, most people would not recognize any spiritual side to what was happening, but Derek felt his ears tingling. Was the world about to be transformed even though most of the population would be unaware of God's presence at the moment?

Derek headed into the park and to the special picnic area where his original encounter took place. He could not imagine why either the visitors, or God, for that matter, would choose him as some special participant in what was happening, but he wanted to be alert just in case.

As he stepped off the path, he again felt a strange warmth come over him and a light descending on him.

"Welcome back, human one. We have a question for you. One of our crew members has a young one, what you call a child. The child remembers reading a legend about a visit to this planet that took place over twenty of our generations ago, about 2,000 or so of your years, in a small village called Nazareth. He made his dad promise that he would ask if there were any memories of such an event."

Derek was stunned. Then he said, "Is this some type of joke or trick question?"

"Please explain yourself, human one."

"There is a village in what we call the Middle East named Nazareth, and something did happen there about 2,000 years ago, but I doubt if it would have been part of a legend on your planet."

"Did it have anything to do with a boy named John?"

Derek looked around to see if some pranksters were nearby.

The voice continued, ". . . and did this boy named John play with another boy? The legend says his name was something like Jesus or something like that."

"All right now, the fun is over. Show yourself." He paused and looked around, trying to spot the source of the voice. Then he was aware that the voice came from inside his head and not some outside source.

He spoke cautiously. "There was a John who grew up in Nazareth, and he had a cousin named Jesus, just about a year younger, that he played with."

"Then our legend has some basis? John and Jesus grew up together in the same small village? Our legend says that as a little boy, this Jesus would make birds out of clay from the water's edge, and when he was finished, he would throw them up into the air, and they would fly away. Is that true?"

"I don't know for sure, but I think that is probably fanciful ideas that often get woven into legends at a later date."

"We also heard that they both got killed by the people in power."

"That part is true. John went around denouncing people's evil deeds, and he denounced one too many people in power, and they had him arrested and eventually executed."

"What happened to the Jesus fellow?"

"He tried to live his life in a way that demonstrated that each individual had value. Regardless of who a person was or what he had done, Jesus tried to love him or her into wholeness."

"That should have made him very popular."

"To some people, but not to everyone. He always started with those who were weakest or most troubled, and sometimes, in the process, he broke some religious laws and traditions if they interfered with the healing. For example, he would heal on the sabbath or denounce how people used religious tradition to shame others. And he taught through storytelling that we should always be generous to others and live in a manner that suggested that all of us, even the worst sinners, were loved by God. He told his listeners that we should offer such love to others, including the worst of sinners. He even deliberately included foreigners and sought out people like tax collectors whom people didn't like."

"In the end, both the religious and the political leaders joined together to have him executed—They hung him on a cross."

You see, you humans are all about power and protecting yourselves, even at the price of sacrificing others. You tell me that this Jesus fellow believed that everyone had value. In the end, that caused those who thought that power was the most important thing to decide to eliminate him. "

"Well, if that was the end of him, you might be right, but people had misjudged the universe's very nature."

"What do you mean?"

"Jesus trusted the God who created the universe from the beginning. And they believed that life, not death, would triumph. So, he tried to love people into their full wholeness."

"But they still crucified him."

That's right, but God took the cross, which was supposed to be a sign of despair, and transformed it into a sign of hope. Jesus was willing to risk everything for the sake of the potential goodness he saw in others, and God responded to that sacrifice by raising him from the dead."

"God did what?"

"God transformed Jesus' death into a sign that life and love can triumph over death and destruction."

"We will investigate this further, oh human one. If it proves to be true, and this God of yours values you so much that he allowed this Jesus to make this sacrifice, your race may prove more valuable than we have recognized."

"We have always believed that God's work and Jesus' demonstration of the work of God impacted the people who live on this planet. While there are some exceptions, most of us have never considered God to be at work among other life forms in this universe. Maybe a benefit of your visit was to learn of this faith from this planet and carry it back to your populations."

"Why would your God do that?"

"Maybe because your ultimate origin is from the same God we serve."

CHAPTER 24
AN OPEN FUTURE

They were so engaged in feelings of joy that had long been neglected that no one was looking up at the saucers in the sky.

It was a child who first cried out. "Momma, look up in the sky. What are those creatures doing?"

You could feel the mood change like a great wave sweeping across the stadium. "Look, they are moving and making strange sounds."

Is it happening? Are they finally going to land? thought Eleanor. She felt a tremor in her stomach and watched as the ships began to take new formations. A central ship seemed to take control and moved closer to the planet. Then a great light lowered itself into the stadium.

Some people did panic, but most watched in stunned silence. They had been preparing for this moment since the saucers first appeared, but now it was here. A strange musical sound and unusual but festive bands of colors filled the sky.

Felicity yelled out in ecstasy. "Woo Woo, Wonderama, are you coming to visit us?"

"Wait, Felicity, first, we must see how they are going to act now that they are landing."

"But, Dad, Woo Woo, and Wonderama are my friends. You saw their picture."

"We saw it, and we have hope, but we must see how they behave. Remember, a wild lion might look friendly, and yet, because it is frightened and doesn't know how we will react, it might attack first."

Felicity turned towards the light as if she were talking to a friend. "We're not lions, Woo Woo. Just act friendly, and we can have a great adventure together."

As the surreal light made contact with the field, some shadowy figures moved within the light. Then a voice began to speak in the light. "We are concerned that our real appearance might frighten you. We are still making adjustments to make our appearance seem more acceptable in the future. The children's music and paintings make us feel welcome in this city. Thank you.

"You have many languages spoken on your planet. We are trying to learn them all, but in the meantime, we will speak in the languages that seem to dominate each population. Have patience and ask us to explain further if you don't understand."

Another voice spoke up: "In honor of Barrie and Felicity's efforts, we will set up a place for hot fudge sundaes and hot dogs at the end of the field. We'd never tasted ice cream before. That is a real treat."

While this exchange was going on, Eleanor stepped forward.

"I am the mayor of this city. If you wish to speak to someone in charge, speak to me," She continued, "Since we have been isolated for almost four earth years in this bubble you've created, we also want to know what is happening in the other cities around the planet."

"Different cities and different cultures have been offered the same opportunity. Their behavior will be reported to the Universe Council. Some have responded better than others."

Eleanor forced herself to remain calm. "Please report to your Universe Council the following. Even as we seek to welcome you as a neighbor, those other cities are also our neighbors. In the same way that you would want us to respond to you with justice, kindness, and mercy, so we ask you to do the same for them."

There were several strange sounds as several light figures seemed almost to bump into each other. After several minutes of what appeared to be exchanges, the initial voice came back. "We did not ask for you to tell us how we should respond? We are under instruction from the Universe Council."

"We didn't invite you to this planet, either. Rather, when you chose to come, we attempted to make you welcome so that we might better understand each other.

"Even though I've never been off this planet, I'm reminding you of the qualities that contribute to positive relationships. I don't have the power to make you do anything, but I can remind you of the best in you."

Again, a voice responded, "If we invited you as mayor of this city to come into our light and be lifted for a brief consultation, are you willing to come?"

Once again, Eleanor reminded herself that she was the one who decided how she would respond. The crowd was silent all over the field, awaiting her response.

"If you are also serving hot fudge sundaes for adults, I'd be pleased to share one with you."

"The crowd burst out in laughter as Eleanor left the hushed crowd around her and slowly began to advance toward the light in the center of the field. In one hand, she held a replica of Felicity's image of the round ball with extended legs; in the other, she held a large red apple.

Without visible trembling, Eleanor stepped into the light. It was a comfortably warm light. There seemed to be figures moving around within it, but none approached her.

For a person who had known the anxiety and fear of hostile prejudice around her throughout her life, she was surprised by a deep sense of being welcome. Whether it was from the last exchange or some other reason, she felt she was being offered respect.

"With your permission," another voice continued, "we will lift you up onto the ship. You may return at any time you desire. Our measure of Earth's worthiness is complete and has been sent to our Universe Council for their decision. If the other cities measure half as well as your city, you have no reason for concern.

"We still have much that we want to learn from you. We are especially interested in how your planet has handled the diversity among your populations. Most of our planets are populated by one or, at most, two distinct groups.

"We also want to learn more about your faiths and how they relate to each other. We especially want to hear about this Jesus who seems to be central to Christianity."

Eleanor considered her response. "We believe that one universal God created all of us – including residents of other planets as well. As part of our being created as beings on this planet, we have diversity buried deep in our hearts. God gives us the freedom to think for ourselves.

"Many times, we have made a mess of it, but God is such a transforming power that God patiently seeks to love us into a rich, diverse wholeness."

"And yet, you have a history of being divided by selfishness, greed, and violence. In our case, you chose to shoot missiles and guns at us."

"Our history is filled with shameful behavior, and if our future depended on our perfection, we would fail miserably, but we believe God, not humans, is the source of our hope."

"Eleanor, you are different from other members of your

Council. We have read about the history of what you call racism. Tell us about yourself. If we gave you the power, how would you want to respond to all those who have treated you and your family with prejudice and discrimination over the past generations?"

Eleanor thought of the grandfather she loved so deeply and how one night, a crowd came and hung him on a tree and ran her family out of town. She had been a victim of intolerance and bigotry all her life. She had learned to cope with it, but the pain deeply scared her life. Now, she was being offered an opportunity to punish those who had done the same to others.

For the first time, she understood with some depth the conflict that people like Nelson Mandela and Desmond Tutu experienced when the power shifted from whites to blacks in South Africa. These technologically superior visitors were not invested in our planet's racial history. Yet, they were offering her the opportunity to bring balance to the injustice that she and her people had experienced for over 400 years. Here was an opportunity to exact reparations for all her ancestors and people.

The crowd held their breath in stunned silence.

"Before I answer that, I must respond to your second question. You said you also wanted to know more about our Christian faith and Jesus."

"Yes, he who was a friend of the one you called John, the

Baptist—his cousin, actually."

"I'm not a learned scholar about either man, but I have experienced this Jesus as personally having given me the courage not to allow the injustices and intolerances of others to determine the shape of my life.

"As I read about him in the Bible or Scripture, he was a man who refused to be shaped by the narrower experiences of either one's physical conditions or one's fears and selfishness. Nor did he allow people's hate or revenge to shape him. He tried to provide examples of how humans can express God's love even in an imperfect world."

"But doesn't basic fairness encourage others to pay a price for their behavior?"

"Many of our residents in both this city and others have a divine generosity planted in their souls, but they are also shaped by their fears and the temptation to focus on their needs rather than on what is best for their neighbors.

"I come from over four-hundred years of being the victim of prejudice. I've been the mayor of this city for several years. Despite being mayor, I've experienced prejudice and intolerance. I've been cursed to my face.

However, in the last couple of years, we can be better humans by listening deeply to others and responding to their needs."

"But the basic logic of fairness . . ."

"Who defines fairness? Usually, it is defined by those who have the most power. How would you like it if my council defined fairness not only for the residents but also for all those of you in the ships that hover above?"

"We have weapons that could destroy this city in a few hours. We don't even know what your concept of fairness is. How could we possibly allow that?"

"So, you are saying that because you have superior power, you get to define fairness. That's hardly fair, is it?"

After a pause, Eleanor continued, "You say that you are evaluating us, but both of us are measuring each other. Can humans and non-humans commit so deeply to the needs of each other that the whole universe will benefit? When we are confident that we will only choose to act in ways that benefit the others, will we have sufficient peace to release the true dimensions of our rich diversity?

"There is no way to prove the other person's intention. We have to be willing to become vulnerable to others who are very different from us. Since I entered the ship, you have called me by name, which in one way is very respectful, but you haven't been willing to risk telling me your names."

"Your appearance may be frightening to us, and yet you could see us and what we look like. What does that assumption say about what you think of us?

The figures in the light beams seemed to stare at Eleanor

in silence as she turned and walked out of the light and back towards those who waited in the field.

On her way, she was interrupted by an excited Felicity, who came running up with a large hot-fudge sundae and an even bigger apple.

"Here, Madame Mayor, you were wonderful. Now stop and rest and treat yourself."

THE END

OTHER PUBLICATIONS BY
Stephen McCutchan

www.smccutchan.com

HEALTHY CLERGY MAKE HEALTHY CONGREGATIONS
Nine-Volume series

1. A Company of Pastors offers a fresh approach to overcoming the type of loneliness that seems inherent in the lives of religious leaders.
   bit.ly/CompanyofPastors

2. An Interim Pastor's Gift recognizes that an interim is the right person to educate a congregation not only on the challenges of ministry but also on ways a congregation can join the pastor to maintain a healthy ministry.
   bit.ly/InterimGift

3. God Laughs—Why Don't You? Introduces the art of humor as a healing antidote to the toxic aspects of ministry so that the clergy can both sustain their own health and offer a

healthy presence to those around them.

bit.ly/Godlaughs

Volume 4, Clergy Physical Health, addresses the physical aspects of health that are affected by stresses and challenges in ministry.

http://bit.ly/clergyphysicalhealth

Volume 5, Clergy Emotional Health, focuses on the way ministry can affect a person's emotional health and contribute to behavior that weakens the ministry

http://bit.ly/clergyemotionalhealth

Volume 6, Clergy Family Health, recognizes that the nature of ministry often is hard on other family members and relationships.

http://bit.ly/clergyfamilyhealth

Volume 7, Clergy Financial Health, recognizes the stress that finances and low salaries can add to a pastor's health. It offers strategies for how to examine and respond to the effect of finances on one's ministry

http://bit.ly/ClergyFinancialHealth

Volume 8, Clergy Spiritual Health, addresses how we can

avoid having the various challenges and stresses of ministry damage our spiritual health. The hidden temptations of a call to ministry are examined.

https://www.amazon.com/dp/B0891ZR1MD

Volume 9, Clergy Vocational Health, looks at both our understanding of the call of God and how to nurture that call even when we have negative experiences.

http://bit.ly/Clergycall

Additional Booklets supporting clergy and the church

PRACTICAL ISSUES AND INNOVATIVE STRATEGIES IN MINISTRY available at www.smccutchan.com

A two-year plan for a Judicatory to shape a culture of Care.

http://bit.ly/2yrPlanclergyhealth

When a church experiences an unhealthy disruption in leadership

http://bit.ly/SadEnd--HealthyBegin

How to Use Technology to unite the church across the miles
http://bit.ly/OneBodyofChrist

How to use writing Fiction to explore spiritual reality
http://bit.ly/Fiction--SpiritualReality

Being a pastor to an Anxious Congregation
http://bit.ly/HealthyClergyMakeHealthyCongregations

A Healthy Response to Grief for congregations
http://bit.ly/AlwaysNewBeginning

How to speak of faith to the Spiritual but Not Religious
http://bit.ly/Salvinchurch

Healthy Clergy Make Healthy Congregations: This program is designed to assist a judicatory in implementing a judicatory-wide program.

One Body of Christ: Offers you a unique way to take advantage of technology to build community with other churches around the world.

Using Fiction to Explore Spirituality: Explore our inner life and build community in a fractured world.

Being Pastor in an Anxious Society: How we can nurture healthy spiritual leadership and provide renewed hope and courage in our anxious society.

Always a New Beginning: a guide to navigate the inevitable losses not as a shrinking of the options but a hopeful anticipation of the new ways that may yet emerge.

Loneliness: an Invisible Virus that needs to be addressed in the ministry.

Sad Endings & Healthy Beginnings: guiding a congregation and former pastor in achieving healthy closure and fresh beginnings.

NOVELS

Exploring the ministry through fictional tales

Clergy Tails—Tales: A series of short stories about clergy in both their noble and shadow sides.

bit.ly/3volClergyTales

A Star and a Tear: A novel wrestling with the interactions between Sexuality and Spirituality.

amzn.to/13VO446

Blessed Are the Peacemakers A novel that addresses faiths response to violence in society http://bit.ly/BlessPeace

Shock and Awe: A novel that explores how the church addresses racism.

https://www.amazon.com/dp/B08ZBJG1PZ

Racism:

Shock and Awe: How the Church Could End Racism in the United States.

Hospitality for Alien Strangers: A novel that reflects on how a community forms its values. Published Oct. 2023

NON-FICTION

Racism and God's Invitation: Our faith invites us to move beyond Denial and Guilt.

https://www.amazon.com/dp/B08FRSXKV8

Racism and God's Grace: Truth and Reconciliation for American Churches

https://www.amazon.com/dp/B08FRSXKV8

Let's Have Lunch: Celebrating 20 years of Presbyterian

Inter-racial dialogue. amzn.to/12ErVoL

Anti-racism Coaching: https://1drv.ms/b/s!Aq75QccEdNd_hNgULaIPWPHCiukm3Q?e=VnCUsB

Spirituality:

Experiencing the Psalm: Prayers that bring the full range of emotions to God in worship. www.helwys.com

Good News for a Fractured Society: divisions of power, wealth, gender, and religious pluralism.

http://bit.ly/GNFractSoc

www.good-news-online.thinkific.com

Is There Salvation in the Church: How God's Saving Power functions in the Institutional Church. http://bit.ly/Salvinchurch

A FINAL WORD

Each of my four novels

1. A Star and a Tear
2. Blessed Are the Peacemakers
3. Shock and Awe
4. Hospitality for Alien Strangers

Are attempts to challenge Christians to explore how real and complex societal issues can be addressed by our faith. You will do me a great favor by joining the conversation through reading and discussing the novels and writing reviews of them for Amazon. https://www.amazon.com/ryp

The more reviews each novel gets, Amazon increases their visibility, and more people engage in the conversation. At its best, Christianity is a faith of relationships in which we don't try to be perfect, but we do try to listen to God and neighbor in a relationship of love and faithfulness.

Thank you for being you, and may you be a blessing to the many people to whom you relate. If you want to continue our conversation, you may reach me at steve@smccutchan.com

Manufactured by Amazon.ca
Bolton, ON

37652115R00111